The State of
Stony Lonesome

Books by Jessamyn West

Jessamyn West

HARCOURT BRACE JOVANOVICH, PUBLISHERS

The State of
Stony Lonesome

SAN DIEGO   NEW YORK   LONDON

Requests for permission to make copies of any part of the work should be mailed to: Permissions, Harcourt Brace Jovanovich, Publishers, Orlando, Florida 32887

Library of Congress Cataloging in Publication Data
West, Jessamyn.
   The state of Stony Lonesome.
   I. Title.
PS3545.E8315S7   1984   813'.54   84–12882
ISBN 0–15–184903–X

Designed by Dalia Hartman

Printed in the United States of America

B C D E

With love for Max

Vista
1921

My uncle Zen's house was up next to the hills in the midst of his scraggly lemon grove. Scraggly because he hadn't been well enough recently to keep it properly irrigated and cultivated, and because he had bought where he thought oil would be, at the edge of the hills, where the soil was thin and shaly. He had signed a lease or two with petroleum speculators and had lived the hopeful life of a man who may be sitting on a gusher. But thus far no drillers had invaded the peaceable landscape to seek the liquid treasure below. Now he contended he was dying, and if there was oil under the place he was no longer sitting on it but lying flat on his back above it.

I drove slowly along the narrow blacktop road between the groves, climbing north and watching the August heat waves rise above the foothills like visible exhalations of crouched and panting animals. Zen's house was the last on the road, the last before the fruit groves, having lost their vigor some hundred yards up the hill's first easy slopes, gave way to what had always been there: cactus, sagebrush, and winter's green grass bleached now in August, bone-dry and bone-colored.

Zen's house was not so much tumbled-down as built slapstick in the first place. If anything, it was firmer now than when he put it up. Zen had not been building for the ages; his house was temporary. All are, of course, but householders fret about them and don't see the bulldozers of the next generation, or the winds of time blowing sand across their tidy doorsills. I don't know whether Zen saw that or not, but he had in any case thrown up a temporary shelter only, just enough boards just close enough together to keep out the Santa Ana and the winter rains.

Anyone who has lived in one of those California ranch bungalows built around 1915 can step blindfolded into any other, get a glass of water in the kitchen, wash his hands in the bathroom, and lie down for a snooze in the back bedroom without ever missing a doorknob or a faucet. They are all alike—a rectangular box divided into six spaces. The three spaces on the right-hand side of Zen's house were front porch, living-dining room, kitchen. The three on the left-hand side were front bedroom, bath, and back bedroom. Zen was spending what he claimed were his last days in the front bedroom of his house because a door opened out of it onto the porch, giving him the benefit of any breeze and a view of the hills.

When he first built here outside the town of Valencia, Zen had done some planting around the house, but from first to last he was no horticulturist. He knew whiskies, tobaccos (smoking and chewing), women, horses, automobiles, and even a few books: *Ships That Pass in the Night, Blix, Castle Craneycrow*. But flowers, no. Nevertheless, he planted, and when he irrigated the grove, he irrigated the flowers. The California sun had done the rest. The bungalow need never have had a nail put into it. Bougainvillaea, lantana, head-high geraniums, Gold of Ophir roses, honeysuckle, poinsettia—these so propped up the house of redwood planks that it existed inside this growth like a clam in a shell. Probably the entire structure could have been eased away, plank by plank, and a bungalow-shaped cavern of firm green would have been left behind.

What mingled there, Zen had no idea. This did not decrease his pride. He had never intended or even anticipated the production of any such bower, and *that* was why he relished it so much. Plant a bower and get a bower? What kind of a story was that? He was nourished by irony and reverses: the cat who tried to dig a hole in the hot tin roof; the wolf in grandma's bed who didn't recognize a fellow beast under Red Riding Hood's hood. He was a great storyteller, but in his repertoire there were no accounts of bowers designed as bowers. Something had spoiled him for the expected.

No evil genius of the tract designer had imposed conformity upon us. We asked for it. Even while we were free and could choose, we chose to be alike.

Zen's house, like those I had been passing—oh, there was an occasional nonconformist Swiss chalet or a two-story throwback to some Midwestern farmhouse—was the familiar rectangular box. While each had a front porch, these porches were rarely used. The people who had built them were Easterners, accustomed to sultry weather and without automobiles. In Ohio or Iowa, if you wanted some air or a view, you sat on the porch. In a California bungalow, the air was soughing through the house anyway, night and day. The weather was never sultry, and if it was a view you wanted, you got into the family car and took a spin.

But houses, whatever their builders may think of the

future, are designed from memory. (What isn't? you may ask.) So it was memory, not need, that tacked on a porch to the California bungalow.

Zen, when he first saw the lushness of his bower, belittled it. I have an idea that with me he was sometimes profane. The wonder and excitement of what he was saying required an occasional narrative respite. To disguise these moments when awe took hold of him, he filled in with a cussword. Sounds thus continued to flow unbroken from him, but *he* had a moment in which to savor the strangeness of it all. With women, however, Zen never swore—though he had the same need to slow and exult. There would be, when he talked to a woman, a little pause, some slight interior rumbling as he unmeshed the cussword gear and threw his conversational mechanism into reverse. Sometimes I wondered if he wouldn't strip both gears, cuss and noncuss, trying too late or too quickly to make a change.

Of his bower, he would say to me, "Why, I hate flowers, Aunt Jetty. I stuck two geranium twigs in the ground to please Love." (Love was his first sweetheart's name.) "Never watered them. Get them started, and a geranium will drink as much as a horse. Love may've watered them on the sly, but I sure as . . . Sam Gopher . . . never carried them a bucket of water myself. The rest of the stuff? Search me. A bird took a rest on one of those geraniums and while there spit out a seed. Up it come. Up some more come. Ringed me round because I don't give a good . . . goldarn . . . about flowers. Why, I'm living in a . . . festering . . . oasis. That's the word for it. Pansies and heliotropes!"

He made the words sound like good juicy blasphemies.

As far back as I can remember, my uncle Zen had called me Aunt Jetty. No one else did, and no wonder. My name is Ginerva. It's natural enough to ease that to Ginny. But Jetty? That's far-fetched. And more so by tagging "Aunt" on the front. Still, it was Zen's gift to me, a sign of distinction from a grown man to his unworldly niece, eighteen years younger than he. I accepted it gladly.

I did not dare return Zen's gift to me with a special name for him. My mother would tolerate no such youthful audacity. So I spoke properly to and of Uncle Zen and Mama and Papa. But in the scenes woven in my mind, I thought of them as Zen and Birdeen and Reno. By those names they were players in my imagined dramas.

I drove out to Zen's almost every afternoon when he was bedfast with a setback. Zen had been in California "curing" when Neddie and I were born. He came home from California, but not "cured." Tubercular patients are never "cured"; the best they can hope for is to have their disease "arrested." That's what happened to him. He came home to Indiana "arrested," like a lucky criminal.

He returned to California later, became an automobile dealer—he sold Hupmobiles—and bought his ranch, with its promise (never kept) of oil.

By the time my father and mother, with their children, reached California, Zen was the leading auto dealer in Orange County. Although laid up now and then with a setback, he had enough energy between these rest periods to outsell all Fords, Maxwells, Studebakers, and Chevrolets in the county.

Zen had heard my car and his eyes were turned toward me as I crossed the porch and entered his room.

"Come out to say good-bye?" he asked me.

I fumbled about for an answer. "I'm not going anyplace."

"I am," he said.

I ignored this. "I came out to see how you were."

"Comfortable as a man can be in my position."

He looked comfortable: clean white nightshirt, three pillows behind his back, Enoch, the big tiger-striped tomcat, spread across his thighs. He was rubbing the fur around the cat's ears, and the look on his face—Zen's—showed how much pleasure he could still get out of touch.

"Pull up a rocker," he told me. "You'll be looking down at me soon enough."

I put the rocker at the foot of the bed so that he could see me without twisting his neck. The room was filled with the scent of geraniums—not a fragrance exactly, but a thick, juicy pungency. Geraniums ordinarily have no scent unless crushed, but the sun on them was heavy enough to cook a smell out of them. In spite of the heat, Zen had three quilts over him, and his face, under the heavy upspring of prematurely graying hair, was bone-colored.

Zen's only sister was my mother. He had affected her —though not in the same way—as vividly as he affected me. She had talked to me a lot about him. She thought him a bad man, though she loved him. The point is, Zen was not just a man. I had done considerable speculating about him. My mother was deeply involved in her emotions about her brother, and it has been my fate to be drawn to the objects and persons and causes enhanced by my mother's emotions. The reason for this, I don't know —unless it is that I so transformed them by my feeling that everything I was ever able to discover for myself seemed by contrast bare and flat. In any case, now, as always, I talked to Zen with the impression that back of all we said there existed some bond that made conversation extremely easy, and sometimes even unnecessary.

So I sat and rocked without speaking, and Zen rubbed Enoch's ears, and through the open door the hills' outlines were blurred in the simmer of heat waves.

"Aunt Jetty," he said, "how would you like to go walking with me?"

Zen's relapses could last as long as six weeks, and never less than three. This one looked like the longer stretch.

"Not today," I said. "You'll be up soon enough, and then we'll go walking and make up for lost time."

"Why not today? We could walk memory right now."

"Walk memory?" I had no idea what Zen meant, but his eyes had turned toward me and were alive with sudden delight.

"Sure. Wander in the past. Stories about my life, and you'll be in them. Stories about yours, and likely I'll be there. There might be some surprises."

Then we remembered together.

Walk Memory 1915

1

It was September 1915. We had been in Valencia, California a few years. September in California has always been a mixed-up time. Summer supposedly over, but inevitably days that bring the year's hottest weather. Crops finishing, schools beginning; the rancid smell of bruised tomatoes mingling with the sweet and heavy scent of Gold of Ophir roses. Green-white winter onions being planted and green-brown English walnuts being knocked off the already yellowing trees by shakers with iron hooks on the ends of their ten-foot poles.

Before schools opened, whole families crawled around under the big bowery trees picking up the fallen walnuts. Pay was by the sack. The owners didn't care if a father wanted to put his two-year-old to work. The child couldn't do any harm, and crawling still came natural at that age.

Reno Chalmers, my father, didn't have a two-year-old. His youngest was Ramona, aged four. Ramona was there with the rest of the family—Neddie, aged seven, and me, aged twelve. My mother, Birdeen, was there, of course; she was thirty-two. Picking up walnuts had been her idea, not Reno's. It wasn't that Reno was averse to work, but he had his own job, caring for the ranches of absentee owners. Birdeen pointed out to him that by getting to his regular work before breakfast and by continuing it after supper, the whole family could sandwich in a week of walnut picking before the school term began. Reno objected some, but he couldn't object too much. If he hadn't bought such a fancy team and wagon, we wouldn't have been so hard-pressed for money.

Crawling around, dusty and sweaty, trying to separate walnuts from clods, I blamed Mama for my predicament. I would have to start school with hands as brown as a Mexican's.

"Papa didn't want us to come out here and pick walnuts," I told Mama. My knees were as wrinkled as walnut hulls from a morning's crawling, and my hair was full of twigs and leaves.

Birdeen answered without stopping work. "Papa is a Chalmers. He will always buy first and figure out how to pay afterward."

This was an old story. I supposed it was true, but it didn't cheer me any. "I guess I'm a Chalmers, too," I said contemptuously.

"Don't you ever say that," Birdeen told me. "You're a McManus if I ever saw one. You're my mother over again. Papa is a fine man. He takes after the Vawters in most ways, but he picked up some of old Tom Chalmers's shiftless ways before he broke loose from home."

"Maybe I'm shiftless," I persisted. "I feel shiftless."

"Never," Birdeen said. "Why, you want a piano as much as I do, Ginerva. Think how it will be. The parlor sweet and clean. Curtains lifting in the breeze. Almost, but not quite, time to turn on the lights. You at the piano playing 'Star of the East.' "

Ordinarily my mother was able to mesmerize me with such imaginings. When I was tired of hanging out diapers for my mother, Birdeen would cry, "Diapers! Snowflakes! Look at them against the sky."

14

When I was daunted by a sinkful of dishes, Birdeen would slip her wedding ring (I was a big girl and Birdeen a little woman) over my finger. "Listen to the music you can make with this. Golden wedding-ring music. The faster you go, the merrier the music."

Such suggestions usually worked. I hung out snow-flakes. I played gold wedding-ring music. But I couldn't, with the sweat running down my face, get myself anywhere near that cool, music-filled parlor at twilight. All I could do was throw walnuts into the bucket faster. In the matter of fastness, anyway, I was certainly no Chalmers. Birdeen and I could fill two sacks to Reno's one, even though he had the help of both Neddie and Ramona. But both of them, of course, were Chalmerses.

The walnut stain on my hands stayed even longer than I had expected. On Friday, after school had been in session for five days, the insides of my hands were still dirty-looking. The kids, going home from school that day, lolloped all over the road. Eventually bored with vacation, we had waited for school to begin. One week of school and we acted like jailbirds after a successful prison break. Anything tickled us; jokes that would have fallen flat on Tuesday or Wednesday doubled us up on Friday.

Dell O'Dell, who had picked up walnuts in his father's grove, held up his hand with a make-believe cigarette between his fingers.

"Darn these cigarette stains," he said. "They give me away every time."

The Rimpo girls, Neddie, and Dell's younger brother Virgil laughed like fools at this. Dell looked at me; I was walking apart from the others along the rose hedge that bordered the road. My fingers were as brown as Dell's. I didn't blame him for trying to be funny. It was the kids I blamed, for pretending that he had succeeded.

"Why don't you chew, then?" I asked Dell.

My nose was out of joint. I had suggested a guessing game to the kids. Along the blacktop road we were following, a fence supported mingled stands of red and white roses. The red roses smelled deep and musky, the white ones, delicate and spicy.

"Let's make a test," I had urged. "Smell with our eyes shut and see if we can tell red from white!"

"Why?" asked Dell.

I didn't know why, except that I loved joint enterprises and this was something we could do together.

"Old Boston Blackie Chalmers, the detective," Dell yelled.

The kids laughed as if he were another Fatty Arbuckle.

"Nose of a bloodhound, mind of a child."

Dell O'Dell was thirteen years old. He had bright blue eyes that glittered like those of someone driving a red car too fast.

"Old Boston Blackie Chalmers," the kids echoed.

After that, I had stayed close to the rose hedge, and played the game by myself. The sun had softened the tar on the road, and when I drew a deep breath, I smelled oil as much as roses. But I never missed with the roses: red, white, red, red. I was right every time. I couldn't keep from calling the results across to the others, not boasting, but still hoping to get them to play with me. "I haven't missed once," I told them.

No one paid any attention, except for Dell O'Dell. He yelled, "Smarty, smarty, had a party, / No one came but a big fat darky."

I buried my face in a rose, pretending to test its smell. I tested and tested until my eyes were dry again. It wasn't what Dell had said. I was used to him. I had gotten up blue that morning. I didn't know why.

"Ginerva," Birdeen had asked, while she combed my hair, "are you still taking on over this apron?"

Birdeen had made me long-sleeved, high-necked aprons to wear to school so that my dresses would stay clean and not wear out. No one else wore aprons to school. "They'll laugh at me," I had told my mother.

"They will not," Birdeen had replied. "You've got too much spunk for that. You'll stare them down."

By Friday I had done so. So it wasn't my apron that was making me unhappy.

"I just got out of bed blue," I had told my mother. "I don't know why."

Mama understood that. I felt the brush strokes soften. Named difficulties, Birdeen made light of. Step on a rusty nail, sneeze your head off, go to school togged out like a scarecrow: Birdeen expected her children to overcome little troubles like those. But nameless sorrow, a heavy heart, or a longing for something, you didn't know what; if that was your trouble, Birdeen bestirred herself.

"Ginerva," she had said, beginning to brush again

with her accustomed vigor, "listen while I recite my piece for tomorrow night. You know it as well as I do. Prompt me if I forget. Tell me if I'm too loud or too fast. Or don't have enough expression."

I was completely taken in. I had to put away my nameless sorrow for Mama's sake. Birdeen was entered in the elocution contest sponsored by the Valencia branch of the Women's Christian Temperance Union. As a girl back East, Birdeen had been an elocution star. The house was filled with prizes she had won: hand-blown paperweights, hand-painted hair receivers, *The Dolly Dialogues* in white leather, title in gold leaf. She was a born reciter, perhaps even an actress. There was a marked resemblance between Birdeen and Sarah Bernhardt; and Birdeen must have known it, for she frizzed her hair in an exact copy of Bernhardt's. Since her marriage, Birdeen hadn't had time or, in California, the opportunity for elocution. Now, with a contest to be held in the church to forward the cause of temperance, it was her duty to perform.

That morning, listening to Mama recite "Kentucky Belle," I had forgotten my blues and hadn't thought of them again until Dell O'Dell sang his mean song.

I listened to the sounds of cars coming from behind me, and since the kids wouldn't play with me, I played another game with myself: Guess which cars are big and expensive from the sounds their tires make on the warm asphalt. I was almost always right: Winstons, Packards, Graham Paiges approached with a rich thick sizzle. Poor little Fords and Maxwells came along quietly, as if ashamed.

I had really forgotten the others, when Alma Rimpo called to me, "Ginerva, Neddie's chewing tar."

When the sun was warm enough to soften the asphalt, almost everyone pried up lumps to chew. Only the Chalmers children were forbidden to. Birdeen, who had no fear of rusty nails or snakebite, was against tar chewing because it wasn't nice. She never mentioned health, only niceness.

"It's not nice to pry up a piece of the road and chew it," she told me. "I don't want you children to do it. You keep an eye on Neddie. He's a boy. He'll be especially tempted. First it'll be tar, and the next thing we know he'll take up tobacco. I trust you, Ginerva, to see that Neddie never chews tar."

With the word "trust," Birdeen put her usual hex on me. I didn't care for my role as nursemaid to Neddie, and it made Neddie hate me. He was a fat little boy, tow-haired and curly-headed, a Chalmers and a sweet one. He almost never started anything that was fun without having me stop him because it was my duty.

Alma Rimpo was right. Neddie was dribbling tar juice like a grasshopper in summer. He had a guilty look when I called to him, but it didn't stop his chewing. Tar mesmerized Neddie. It was a big gamble with every chew as to whether he'd be able to pry his jaws open or not. Neddie wanted to keep on gambling, but with me he didn't have a chance. With one hand, I fished the chaw from his mouth; with the other, I mopped his face on a corner of my apron.

"Lick your teeth clean," I ordered him. "They're black."

Neddie, in the way that endeared him to all, cheerfully licked. He hadn't said a word during the entire operation. I, set for an argument, was disappointed.

I turned on Dell. "What do you think you're doing, Dell O'Dell?"

What Dell was doing was as plain as day. With a dried milkweed stalk, he was switching the fat legs of Alma Rimpo's simple-minded sister, Rosie. He couldn't switch hard or the stalk would break. Rosie was giggling and galloping in her pudgy way.

"What I'm doing, Ginerva Chalmers, is driving my fat horse to market. Ain't I, Rosie?"

Dell gave Rosie as sharp a rap as the milkweed stalk would stand. Rosie gave as frolicsome a leap as her fat legs could manage.

"Giddy-ap, Rosie," commanded Dell.

"You stop that, Dell O'Dell," I shouted. "Shame on you."

It would have been different if Rosie hadn't been simple-minded. She was eight, as big as a twelve-year-old, and about as smart as a two-year-old. She still wet her pants, even though Alma took her to the lavatory even between recesses. Half of Dell's fun now was in seeing the round wet spot on the back of Rosie's dress bob up and down like a loose taillight whenever she pranced.

"Get a move on there, Rosie," was Dell's reply.

"You stop picking on Rosie this minute."

"Who says so?" Dell asked, gently switching away.

"I do."

"You and who else?" Dell asked.

"God," I said earnestly.

"God?" Dell asked, not expecting to hear that word on the way home from school.

I wished I could back down. Not that I wasn't sure that God *was* against simple-minded girls having their legs switched on the way home from school; but I didn't want to be the one to tell Dell so. I knew it wasn't brave of me to be unwilling to take a stand for the right, but I was tired from a week of staring kids down who laughed at my apron, without having to stand up for God, too. Especially to Dell O'Dell.

But I *had* to put a stop to the switching. Dell had stopped in his tracks. "Hey," he said, grinning, "I forgot. You got saved at the revival, didn't you?"

Dell wasn't the one to talk about that. He had got half saved himself. He had come down the aisle all the way to the amen bench, crying like a baby. But there he had refused to say a word, so no one could say for sure whether he'd been saved or not.

Dell himself said he wasn't. "I just came down the aisle," he said, "to get a better look at the goings on."

I knew better. He hadn't been pretending there, down front. He was really broken-hearted, but didn't have the courage to take a stand. This was a test, especially planned for me now. I would have to set an example of courage for Dell O'Dell.

I felt the neck of my apron grow tight, but in spite of it I said, "Yes, I was saved." I wondered if it could be true for, while I was saying it, I was speculating about the tire sizzle coming up the road behind me.

Dell didn't argue with me as I had expected. He just nodded his head like some good old preacher.

"Born again," he said reflectively, "born again."

Then he lifted his milkweed stalk and gave Rosie another stroke or two.

"You mustn't," I said. "It's wrong."

"Rosie," Dell asked, "you want to play horse?"

"Yes," Rosie said. "Play horse."

"Want me to whip you, Rosie?"

"Whip the horsie," said Rosie.

"It's wrong," I persisted.

"You heard what Rosie said."

"She doesn't know what she's talking about."

"Ginny," said Dell, "you take Rosie's place and I'll spare Rosie."

I knew it didn't hurt, but still I hesitated. I was as bad as Birdeen. It didn't seem *nice* to stand up in front of a boy and let him switch your legs. There was nothing wrong in it if you couldn't help yourself; or if you didn't know any better, like Rosie. But I knew better.

"I guess you're not as saved as you think," Dell said. "You sure ain't going to lay down your life for your brother."

"All right," I said slowly.

"All right, what?"

"I'll take Rosie's place."

"You want me to switch you?"

"Yes," I said.

"You know what you're talking about, don't you, Ginny?"

"Yes," I said, but I didn't know whether I did or not. I was sure it was wrong for Dell to whip Rosie, but I didn't know whether it was right for me to take Rosie's place.

"Giddy-ap," said Dell, and I began to cry. I was prepared to sacrifice myself, but I couldn't help crying.

"Go on, whip me," I told Dell, when no blows followed.

"I don't switch a crybaby," Dell said. He broke his milkweed stalk in two, and he, with all the kids behind him, raced down the road ahead of me. I was left alone. The cars sizzled by. The asphalt and rose smells mingled. Utterly alone. Blue, blue. No one cared enough about me even to switch my legs.

2

Neddie and I, whose home was the farthest from the school, were alone by the time we reached the Leffingwell arroyo. I was glad we were alone. I had made a fool of myself, and for the last mile no one would speak to me. Trying to keep Dell from switching simple-minded Rosie's legs with a milkweed stalk was a mistake for two reasons: it turned out that Rosie *wanted* her legs switched; then I, when I said I would take Rosie's place, had bawled like a two-year-old at the first lick, even though I wasn't in the least hurt. It was humiliating. The kids despised me, and I didn't blame them.

I didn't know why I had cried, but I knew I wouldn't have if I hadn't gotten up blue that morning. I didn't know why I was blue, either, but all day the shadow of something I could not see, but dreaded, fell over ordinary happenings, darkening them. It made Rosie's simple-mindedness terrible. It made the elocution contest Mama was going to be in the next night fateful, like a battle or a court decision. It made Dell's switching girls' legs with a milkweed stalk nasty. It had made, this shadow, the one soft lick he had given me painful, though it didn't hurt.

Neddie still wasn't talking to me, but this didn't mean that Neddie was mad or disgusted. Neddie never talked, or almost never. He wasn't backward like Rosie Rimpo, or even bashful. I had given up trying to understand Neddie. I wanted to know what other people thought and felt. How could you find out except through talk? Neddie didn't care to find out. He never asked questions and only occasionally volunteered opinions. Sometimes I thought angrily that I had as well have a stone or a cloud for a brother—and sometimes I was glad. Even though he didn't reply, Neddie apparently listened to every word I said. His round blue eyes would change intensity. He would smile or frown or scratch his curly head.

At the arroyo we had to either turn down the road toward our own home or go in the opposite direction along the road that led through the Leffingwell ranch. I didn't feel ready to go home yet.

"Neddie," I said, "let's go down the arroyo."

"Why?" asked Neddie with unexpected responsiveness.

"It'll be cool down there," I said.

It would be cooler, anyway. The September afternoon was hot; the tar on the blacktop road was melting, and the cars went by with the hot-weather whine of tires on soft asphalt. The Leffingwell arroyo wasn't the usual Southern California dry gulch with nothing in it but sand and cactus, horned toads and trap-door spiders, just as the Leffingwell ranch itself wasn't the usual ten or twenty acres, but two hundred and fifty acres of orange and lemon groves, complete with bunkhouses for the men who worked there. The Leffingwell arroyo had been landscaped. A little stream flowing from the ranch reservoir ran at its bottom. The arroyo was roofed over with feathery branches of pepper and acacia trees. Steps down from the road led into another kingdom, a kingdom beneath the earth where there were shadows and ferny smells and the strange sound of running water.

"I'm cool," Neddie said.

I could go without Neddie. Even though I wasn't supposed to leave little brother alone, we were so near home now that unless Neddie walked smack into an automobile on purpose, no harm could come to him. It was for my own sake I wanted Neddie along. I wasn't exactly afraid of the arroyo and its under-earth shadows and smells and sounds, but the fear I did have was more enjoyable if someone was with me.

"We might meet Joe," I said, wheedling.

Joe was the Japanese gardener, the one who had made an underground kingdom of the arroyo. He was the one who had planted the pampas grass, the color of a palomino's tail; and had set out the bamboo shoots, whose leaves, down at the bottom of the windless arroyo, rustled, rustled, with the sound of thirsty sparrows whispering. The bamboo, Joe had said, had three purposes: to look cool; to move even when there was no wind; and to break up the strong bright light of California into little bamboo-shaped pieces that the eyes could play with, without being hurt.

"He might give you some candy," I said, as Neddie stood irresolute, pointed toward neither home nor the arroyo.

"Mama said for you not to eat Joe's candy."

"I'm not going to. If we meet him and he gives us

candy, I'll give all of mine to you. She didn't say you couldn't eat it, did she?"

She hadn't and I didn't know why. When I had asked her, she had answered, shortly, "Because you're a girl."

Papa had objected to this. "You'll just put ideas in her head, Birdeen. Set her to worrying about things she can't understand."

"Better worry than be sorry."

"Come right down to it, Birdeen, she don't have to do either."

"You're a fine one to talk, Reno Chalmers," Mama had said, ending that conversation.

Mama hadn't made me worry, but she had set me to wondering—and to feeling important. When I walked down into the arroyo nowadays, even when I didn't see Joe, which was most of the time, I felt as if the arroyo itself awaited and noticed me; as if it had something to offer me that it could never offer Neddie. Something dangerous, beyond any dangers in Joe's candy, that at its worst could only poison me. Though how Joe could manage a candy that would poison girls, not boys, I couldn't figure out; nor why he would *want* to poison girls. He was the smallest and most polite man I had ever known. He picked flowers and carried them in his hands like a woman. He showed us how stones changed color under water; and asked us to notice that when the bamboo leaves flickered, fish-shaped pieces of sunlight swam past them in the arroyo's green shade. He taught us to suck honey from the nasturtiums and made us be quiet so we

27

could hear the little stream's occasional faint hubbub. He gave us gifts that could not possibly be poisonous: paper lanterns, and kites and little birdcages in which he said we could keep mice or crickets instead of birds, if we wanted to.

It was because of this new threat of the arroyo that I wanted company down there. It was odd that I should want to go where there was a threat, but the threat was part of the pleasure, and would make me forget how silly I had been up there on the road, switched with a milkweed stalk. And it suited my blueness to be down there where the sun was blotted out and all the sounds were muffled and the smells were strange and damp.

Arguing with Neddie sometimes made him mulish. I left the road for the path that led down into the arroyo, as if he had already said yes. My words about the candy had turned the trick; he was right behind me. Neddie roamed the banks, peering down the rows of orange trees for a sight of Joe. I walked along the edge of the stream, which carried red berries from the pepper trees on its surface like offerings to a heathen god. Joe went to the Church Mission School, but maybe he wasn't entirely weaned from his heathen gods. The Leffingwell ranch bell rang for quitting time. It would ring again at six, when all the ranch hands ate. Usually I, pretending that the bell was a chapel bell calling people to prayer, prayed when I heard it ring. This evening, I didn't feel like prayer. Prayer was a going away from yourself toward heaven, and I didn't want to leave myself or the green tunnel or the clear stream carrying its offering of red berries.

I had lost sight of Neddie while listening to the bell and watching the flicker of bamboo fish, and this frightened me—not for myself, but for him. Neddie was my responsibility. I began to call his name, not nearly as loud as I could, because it seemed wrong to scream in the quiet of the arroyo. I walked along searching on both sides of the arroyo for a sight of his white blouse and brown knickerbockers: on the right, where the tree rows of the ranch began; on the left, where the arroyo was bordered by the public road. It was only by chance that, through a clump of oleanders, I saw Neddie coming down toward me from the left, calm and silent. If he had been near enough, I would have given him a shake.

"Didn't you hear me calling you, Neddie Chalmers?"

Neddie nodded.

"Why didn't you answer me?"

"I thought you wanted me to come."

I gritted my teeth. "What've you been doing?"

"Nothing."

"Why were you so quiet?"

"I was watching Papa and a lady."

"Watching them? What are they doing?"

"Nothing," said Neddie.

"Where are they?"

"Down the road a ways."

I climbed right up to the oleander clump, where by parting the branches I was able to see all that Neddie had seen. It wasn't a very world-shaking sight. Reno sat on the high seat of his wagon, his hat on the back of his head and one foot cocked up on the brake lever. Below him, parasol up to protect her pink-and-white complexion, was

Mrs. Marie Ashton. Mrs. Ashton's parasol was built like a pagoda, layer on layer of embroidered white material, and Mrs. Ashton herself was all in starched white and glistened like a newly iced cake. Her blond hair rose in a springy pompadour, and I could see her rings flash as she twirled her parasol. It was impossible to hear what she and Reno were saying, but I could hear them laughing, especially I could hear Mrs. Ashton. After one prolonged trill, Mrs. Ashton took the tip of her parasol and gave Reno's leg, above the boot top, a playful poke.

The minute she did that, I grabbed Neddie's arm. "My dream, Neddie," I said. "It's just what I dreamed."

It was useless to expect Neddie to ask, "What did you dream, Ginerva?" If you wanted to confess anything to Neddie, you did it on your own hook and could never blame him afterward by saying, "I didn't want to do it, but Neddie coaxed me." I didn't need any coaxing to tell Neddie. My dream came back to me so vividly, I seemed to be living through it all, once again.

"Neddie, you know that song Papa sings all the time, 'Sweet Marie'? That love song?

> " 'In the morn when I awake,
>   Sweet Marie,
> Seems to me my heart will break,
>   Love, for thee.'

You know it, don't you?"

Neddie shook his head.

"He sings it all the time. Why don't you know it?"

"I don't know," Neddie said.

"I don't know how you have sense enough to be in the third grade," I said. "I'm sure glad I'm not your teacher."

"Me, too," said Neddie, surprising me for a second out of the memory of my dream.

"Sure you are. I'd make you learn something if I was your teacher. Do you know what Papa did?"

"In your dream?" Neddie asked. Neddie was terribly undependable.

"In my dream. But you can dream what's true. In the Bible, they did all the time."

Neddie knew better than to question the Bible.

"In my dream, Papa stood up in church and sang that song to Mrs. Marie Ashton. He made the preacher stop preaching and the choir stop singing. Mama was there and I was there and Ramona was there. And *you* were there, Neddie Chalmers. You listened, too."

Neddie looked surprised, but said nothing.

"He bowed to Mrs. Marie Ashton, put his hand over his heart and sang.

" 'I've a secret in my heart,
Sweet Marie.
I've a tale I would impart,
Love, to thee.'

He sang that right before Mama. Mama hid her face, but her tears dropped down onto her white skirt and made big gray splotches."

"What did I do?" asked Neddie.

"Nothing," I snapped. "You sat there like a bump on

a log. So did I," I admitted. "But I suffered and Mama suffered. And Mrs. Marie Ashton just preened herself. She should have been ashamed, but she was proud. They both should have been ashamed. That's why I've been so blue all day. I forgot my dream, but I remembered the badness. That's why I cried when Dell switched my legs. I was crying for Mama."

I took Neddie's hand in mine and began to clamber up the bank, through oleanders and bamboo, and over nasturtiums and geraniums.

"You're hurting me," Neddie protested.

"Don't complain," I said. "It's for Mama."

But when I reached Reno and Mrs. Marie Ashton, I was just as tongue-tied as Neddie. I couldn't very well say, "You were bad in a dream I had." Or "Stop poking my father with your parasol." And especially I couldn't say, "How dare you look so pink and white and cool and rested when my mother's home picking tomatoes with a barley sack tied on for an apron?" But I did what I could. I glared.

"Well, well, look who's here," Reno said, smiling; though not as much as he had been, I noted, before Neddie and I arrived.

"The schoolchildren!" Mrs. Ashton exclaimed, with enough surprise in her voice for camels and elephants. For a minute, I thought Mrs. Ashton was going to give *me* a little poke with her parasol. I braced myself. I didn't intend to let that happen.

"What are you kids doing down here?" Reno asked.

"Going home from school," I answered patiently.

"Aren't you a little off the beaten track?" Before Mrs.

Ashton, Reno was as polite to his children as if he had never laid eyes on us before. I scorned him for it.

"We've been down in the arroyo," I said, testing him a little more. We were supposed to come straight home from school, with no loitering in arroyos or elsewhere.

"Nice and cool down there, I bet," said Reno, the old fourflusher.

"Cooler than where Mama is, picking tomatoes."

That wiped the smile off Reno's face. "Your mother doesn't have to pick tomatoes, Ginerva, and you know that as well as I do. I did my best to persuade her to stay home today."

"I surely can't understand anyone picking tomatoes on a day like this," Mrs. Ashton said, sympathizing with Reno.

"The bills," I explained politely.

I was glad to see that Papa had the grace to color up. He put his hat on straight. He took his foot off the brake. "I better be moseying on, Marie," he said.

"Tell Birdeen to stay out of the tomato patch and save her energy for the contest."

"I've told her," Reno said.

"Tell her what I said about her selection."

"It's a little late to do anything about it—but I'll tell her. Come on, kids. Climb on."

"We're walking," I said.

Reno looked down at me. "Suit yourself," he said coolly and started up his team.

The three of us watched Papa drive away from us down the tree-lined road.

"I wanted to ride," said Neddie.

"Why didn't you say so?" I snapped.

"He's bashful," Mrs. Ashton explained, testing the spring in Neddie's curls with a pink-and-white hand.

"You don't have to be bashful with your own father," I told her.

"You aren't bashful, are you, dear?" asked Mrs. Ashton.

I didn't know about bashful, but I did know I wasn't Mrs. Ashton's dear.

"You were saved at the revival, weren't you, dear?"

At that minute, I did not feel saved. I wished a bell would ring out and call me to prayer.

"The world has changed for you, hasn't it?"

It hadn't a bit. "I am trying to change," I corrected her.

Mrs. Ashton laughed, and I couldn't help admiring the sound. When Birdeen laughed, it was almost as if she were taken with a fit.

"Has big sister changed any, little bubber?" Mrs. Ashton said, pressing Neddie's curls again.

Neddie looked around to see who Mrs. Ashton was talking to.

"Answer," I ordered. "Have I changed?"

"Changed what?"

Mrs. Ashton laughed again. She threw back her head and closed down her lids over her violet eyes; but the sound she made was still delicate and controlled. Then she opened her eyes and gave Neddie a poke with her parasol.

"You poked me in the belly button," Neddie said, surprised, tenderly feeling the spot.

I was heartsick. What would Mrs. Ashton think of a mother who let her children use language like that?

"Neddie picks up bad language at school," I explained.

"If that's the worst, there's not much to worry about."

"My mother would worry if she knew Neddie said 'belly.'"

"Birdeen takes things hard," Mrs. Ashton agreed. "That's why I was asking your father to try to persuade her to change to a temperance recitation for the contest. The judges are picked by the W.C.T.U. They're going to give the preference to temperance pieces."

Mrs. Ashton couldn't tell me anything about the contest that I didn't know. "The rules didn't say it had to be temperance. They just said a ten-minute recitation, and the one who recited best would win."

"I was trying to help Birdeen," Mrs. Ashton said.

"Is your piece about drunkenness?"

"It's about the sin of overindulgence," Mrs. Ashton corrected me.

"Mama doesn't think it will help the cause of temperance to spend a whole evening hearing about drunkards."

I made this up on the spur of the moment. Birdeen was going to recite a Civil War piece because she loved it.

"It's a matter of opinion, I suppose," Mrs. Ashton said. "I thought your mother should know."

"What's the name of your piece?" I asked.

Mrs. Ashton was all smiles again. "'The Tale of a Tramp,'" she said.

She closed her parasol and leaned on it. She shook

all over like a broken old drunkard. Without being asked, she began to recite.

" 'Once I was young and handsome,
　　Had plenty of cash and clothes;
　　That was before I got to tipplin'
　　And gin got in my nose.' "

She was a bad woman, but a wonderful reciter. It was a terrible combination for Birdeen to be up against. If the judges really wanted warnings about strong drink, they couldn't have a better one. Mrs. Marie Ashton collapsed from alcohol before your very eyes. I, who had great confidence in Birdeen's elocutionary powers, was filled with doubt. Was anyone going to care about the Civil War, a young Confederate cavalryman, and a pretty little mare called Kentucky Belle?

"Say some more," said Neddie.

I grasped Neddie's arm in a pinching hold. "Gin gets in your nose?" I asked critically. "That sounds funny. How do you get gin in your nose?"

"It's just a way of speaking," said Mrs. Ashton. "It means the fumes of drink go to your head. That's the way drunkards *are,* dear. The mere smell of it will cause them to commit bloody crimes."

"Mama's piece has nothing to do with bloody crimes. It's all about a young hero and bravery and a noble horse and a dash for freedom."

"This program," said Mrs. Ashton, "is about drink."

It appeared to be a stand-off, but I had no intention

36

of leaving Mrs. Marie Ashton with the last word. As soon as Mrs. Ashton had turned to go on her way down the Leffingwell road, I sang in an offhand, but carrying voice.

> " 'Every daisy in the dell
> Knows my secret, knows it well.
> Yet I cannot, dare not tell
> Sweet Marie.' "

As I sang, I bent over, pretending to be pulling up my stockings; but I was not bent over so far as to be unable to see that Mrs. Marie Ashton, at the first words of the song, stopped in her tracks and turned to watch the Chalmers children. I finished the song, then turned my back on Mrs. Marie Ashton.

"Well," I said grimly to Neddie, "now she knows I know."

"What?" asked Neddie.

"What I dreamed. I told you."

Neddie looked puzzled.

"You don't pay any attention when I talk to you, Neddie. You act like you do, but you don't. You were right there when it happened, and you sat like a bump on a log. And then I explained it to you and you still don't know what happened."

"What happened?"

"See? It's a waste of time to talk to you, Neddie."

We started slowly homeward, the acacias and jacarandas and peppers of the arroyo on one side, the orderly rows of a lemon grove on the other.

Neddie, on the arroyo side, said, "There's Joe down there. He waved to me. Maybe he's got some candy. Let's go down in the arroyo."

"It's too late for Joe now," I told him. "We've got to go home and help Mama."

3

It was eight o'clock of that warm September evening. Everyone except my mother and me had gone to bed. Birdeen was in the kitchen putting cucumber lotion on her hands, and I was in the living room watching her. The kitchen was lighted, and the living room wasn't, so I had the feeling of looking onto a stage—something I had never done, but I had no trouble imagining it. Birdeen was an elocutionist, which is only one step from being an actress. All of her gestures and intonations were desperate and dramatic.

Birdeen had big gray-green eyes and long, though not thick, eyelashes. Her eyes were set in shallow sockets so that they lifted her eyelids when she closed them. Her hair was chestnut with reddish threads. Some people, seeing her in the sunlight, called her a redhead. No one ever called her a redhead more than once. Redheads, in her opinion, were coarse, hot-tempered, and unreliable, none of which Birdeen had any intention of being. She had a lot of hair but it was straight as a stick, slippery as the wind, and not all of her work with a curling iron was able to change this. Her nose was large and a little crooked, and so was her mouth. Her teeth were almost, but not quite, buck. This gave her the look of having something on the tip of her tongue to say—and this, most of the time, was actually the case.

I did not consider Mama good-looking. Reno was the looker in the family. Everyone was agreed on this. Nevertheless, I spent more time looking at my mother than at my father. There was no point in detailing Reno's face. Maybe he was as handsome as a Greek god; but like all the Greek gods I had seen in pictures, his face did not alter from minute to minute. Birdeen's did, especially when she was reciting. When my mother recited, she was "carried away," she "forgot herself." Sometimes this was frightening. Having a changeable mother was interesting, but having a mother who disappeared before your eyes was the next thing to watching her abandon you— or die.

In the kitchen, Birdeen was holding her hands over her head as she massaged them. They were long-fingered, limber as gloves, and, when she wasn't picking tomatoes, white. Except for the bottle of cucumber lotion on the sink, Birdeen might have been in a play. She was lifting her hands to heaven, saying, "What shall I do? What shall I do?" Her lover was at the door. He told her what to do. "Fly with me, my darling. Let me take you away from all this."

There was plenty to fly from. The back porch was stacked with the boxes of tomatoes Birdeen had spent the day picking. Even in the living room, I could smell them, too sweet for a vegetable, too earthy for a flower. The smell went down the back of your throat and stayed there like the taste of something swallowed a long time ago. It was because of the tomato picking that Birdeen had to spend extra time tonight massaging her hands—the juice from the tomato vines made them burn like fire.

When Reno, at the supper table, had seen Mama's hands, red and swollen, he had pushed back his plate.

"Something wrong with the cooking?" Birdeen had asked.

"The cooking's fine. It's your hands."

"They're not a very pretty sight, I know. But I didn't think they were bad enough to make you lose your appetite."

"Birdeen, don't twist things. It's not their looks. It's knowing how they got that way. You out there all day in this heat, bent double, picking tomatoes."

"I didn't do it for you. You know that. I did it because we had—"

"O.K. I know why you did it. But those fellows make a big profit. They don't expect their bills to be paid the minute they mail them. They figure a little waiting in with their costs."

"That's Chalmers talk, if ever I heard it," Birdeen said. "Get what you want and let the other fellow worry about paying."

"That's my motto," Reno said, in a hard, hurt voice.

"I'd be ashamed to admit it before the children."

"Birdeen, I don't mind you bringing up my shortcomings. That's an old story to all—me *and* the kids. But I'd like to put a stop to this crazy tomato picking. You've got your heart set on winning that contest tomorrow night. How do you figure to get up there and recite when you're already so tired you can't hold your head up?"

"I don't have my heart set on winning."

"Skip that, then. You are going to be in it. Why d'you insist on picking tomatoes?"

"They have to be picked when they're ripe."

"They don't have to be picked at all by you. We're

not going to starve for the lack of what you can make picking a dozen boxes of tomatoes."

"Starve! There's more to life than food."

"That's my point. There's this contest. Silver offering for temperance. According to you, temperance is pretty important."

"Just because liquor's never been a temptation to you, Reno Chalmers, don't you run down temperance."

"For God's sake," Reno shouted. "What I'm running down is tomato picking, not temperance."

"Don't curse and yell before the children, Reno."

That was the first time in my life I had ever heard my father take the name of the Lord in vain. I couldn't blame him for getting mad at my mother for talking as if cursing was a habit with him. He had been sitting with his chair tilted back. When Birdeen mentioned cursing, he crashed it down on all four legs, jumped up, and said, "Birdeen, you wanted a scene and you've got one. Now you can pick tomatoes until you fall down in your tracks, and you won't hear another word out of me."

With that, though he hadn't finished his supper and it was barely more than dark, he went upstairs to bed. I knew he wasn't asleep, for I could hear the sound of the bedsprings as he twisted and turned in the room over my head.

I had laid the clothes Birdeen was to wear tomorrow night across a chair. Not because I expected her to put them on but because, if she could see them, it would make the contest more real when she came in to practice: white shirtwaist, lacy with insertion; white ten-gore Indian Head skirt; white high-heeled buck shoes, so clean they reflected the light from the kitchen lamp. The only new thing Birdeen had for the occasion was a pale blue kid belt, worked in seed pearls. It set off her small waist to perfection.

Birdeen, when she saw the clothes laid out on the chair, said, "I'm too tired to put those on, Ginerva."

"I know it," I answered. "I thought you might put on the belt, though."

Birdeen circled her waist with the belt and slowly fastened the buckle.

"It transforms you, Mama."

"I could stand a little transforming."

"Mama, why do you have to pick tomatoes—"

"Ginerva, if you're going to start that, go upstairs with your father. You two can talk tomatoes together."

"I'm not. I won't."

"I oughtn't to have spoken to your father the way I did," Birdeen admitted. "He's a Chalmers and he can't help it."

Birdeen went to the window, which was wide open, and pushed the curtains farther apart. She wasn't feeling playful tonight. All she said was, "Not a breath of air."

"Mama," I said, and then stopped.

"Don't say 'Mama' unless you have something to say."

"I do," I said, and stopped again.

"Well, I can't bring it out of you," Birdeen said.

"I saw Mrs. Marie Ashton on the way home from school."

My mother turned away from the window quickly. "Oh," she said. Then she asked, "Where was she?"

"On the road. She was out for a walk."

"It seems like a pretty hot day for walking."

"She was carrying a parasol. It was covered with embroidery ruffles like a corset cover."

"She carries a parasol, does she?"

"She poked Neddie with it."

"Why, that's dangerous. Any sudden movement and she might put out an eye."

"She poked Papa, too."

"Papa? Where was—Papa?"

"He was on the wagon, coming home from work."

"How could she . . . get at him?"

"He was stopped. Talking to her. And he had one leg kind of out of the wagon on the brake pedal. And when he said anything funny, Mrs. Ashton would laugh and poke him in the leg with her parasol."

"Your father never struck me as being so very funny."

"I couldn't hear what he was saying. I could just see them. Then when Neddie and I got up close enough to hear, Mrs. Ashton didn't laugh so much."

"I never knew your father was such a jokester," Birdeen said again, wonderingly.

"He didn't say anything funny after I got there. Did Papa tell you what Mrs. Ashton said?"

"No," said Birdeen. "He didn't mention seeing Mrs. Ashton."

"She sent a message by him."

"Well, your father failed to deliver it."

"She sent it by me, too. She says that because the contest tomorrow night is put on by the W.C.T.U., the judges will favor pieces about temperance."

Birdeen played with the buckle of her blue kid belt, tightening and untightening it, almost as if she were giving herself artificial respiration.

"The rules don't say a thing about the subject of recitation."

"I know that, Mama. I told Mrs. Ashton that you thought it would be wrong to spend a whole evening, with children present, saying poems about drunkards."

"When did I say that?" Birdeen asked, her voice full of wonder at the wisdom she could utter and forget.

"I don't remember when."

"I used to know a piece called 'Whiskey Joe,'" Birdeen said.

"But, Mama, you love to say 'Kentucky Belle.'"

"I do, I do," Birdeen agreed. "It's fact. I can put my heart into that piece."

"I told Mrs. Ashton that your piece was about an unselfish woman, a brave young man, and a noble horse."

"What's noble about the horse? How do you figure that, Ginerva?"

"He carries the boy to safety."

"What did Mrs. Ashton have to say to that?"

"What could she say?" I asked, feeling Mama's approval.

"Did she mention her recitation?"

"She recited some of it," I said triumphantly. "It's called 'The Tale of a Tramp.' It begins

"'Once I was young and handsome,
  Had plenty of cash and clothes;

That was before I got to tipplin'
And gin got in my nose.' "

I knew exactly what I was doing to Mrs. Marie
Ashton's piece: wrecking it. Mama leaned back against
the window laughing.

"Oh, my gosh, no!" Mama exclaimed, when I
finished. " 'Gin got in my nose,' and all that sniffing and
snuffling. Why, that's sidesplitting."

It hadn't been sidesplitting the way Marie Ashton
had said it. I felt both guilty and relieved. I had made my
mother laugh, which was what I wanted to do. But I
had as good as lied about Mrs. Ashton, too.

" 'Gin got in my nose.' In church? Surely not."

Birdeen walked from the window and lifted her arms
above her head in a big comfortable yawn. "That's the
first time I've been able to straighten up completely since
I came in from picking. Well, that settles it. I'll stick to
'Kentucky Belle.' If the judges want drink, Marie Ashton
can give it to them."

"Give them a noseful," I said daringly, hoping for
another laugh. I didn't get it. Mama went to the window
again, where she twisted the curtain around her arm.

"How did Mrs. Ashton look?"

There was no way to make Mama laugh about Marie
Ashton's looks. "She had too much starch in her dress."

"That tells me a lot."

"You see her at church all the time."

"How did she look today?"

"The same as always."

"Why didn't you and Neddie ride home with your father, if you met him on the road?"

"We didn't want to."

"Did he give Mrs. Ashton a lift?"

"Oh, no. She stayed with us. That's when she recited. Mama, I sang 'Sweet Marie' to Mrs. Ashton."

" 'Sweet Marie'?" my mother asked, as if not understanding what I meant.

"You know.

" 'In the morn when I awake,
     Sweet Marie,
   Seems to me my heart will break,
     Love, for thee.'

I did it to test her. She knows it."

"I don't know what that tests," Mama said. "Everybody knows it. Your father sings it morning, noon, and night. A person would have to be deaf not to know 'Sweet Marie' nowadays."

I was silent for a while. Then I said, "Are you going to practice your piece, Mama?"

"We both know it forward, backward, and sideways," she said. "There's not much point going over it once more."

"I like to hear it."

Birdeen let go of the curtain. She straightened herself, she lifted her head, and an expectancy, an urgency that hadn't been in the room before, entered it. The night wind was beginning to move the curtain behind Birdeen;

the light from the kitchen lamp was reflected from the seed pearls of her belt; the disappearance of my mother began. Birdeen was becoming the Southern girl, frightened, brave, and unselfish. Mystery was enveloping the room. Before her eyes, that which was not took shape. I felt her mind being opened like a book. There were pages in it I had never dreamed of, events to come that were grand and frightening; and moving in and out of these were forgotten memories like gold-and-green fireflies. All this, my mother's words brought to me. They were words I knew as well as my ABC's. But as she spoke them, they rang with the sense of lost jewels and journeys yet to be taken and the priceless gifts of love. They rang with the great names of a bloody war—Old Kentuck and Tennessee, Morgan's Raiders and the Michigan cavalry. The beat of Birdeen's voice slowed to the finish. There was power in it yet, but she was furling it like a flag or easing it like a bird coming home to roost. The war was over. Men had died. But there had been courage and unselfishness, too. I felt as saved as I had at the revival. I felt clean and sweet and ready for the sacrifice.

"Oh, Mama," I said, "that was the best you ever said it. I know you'll win tomorrow night."

Birdeen sighed. She folded her arms across her breast as if the room's slight cooling had chilled her.

"I will do the best I can," she said. "I've worked hard on it. It isn't as if, though," she went on, "I was free to give all my time and energy to it—like Mrs. Ashton."

"Mama," I burst out, "let me—"

"Let you what, Sister?"

"Pick tomatoes tomorrow."

I had been afraid my mother would flare up. But she said calmly, "You look after the house and the children."

The clock on the bookcase struck nine. Upstairs the bed squeaked. Out in the barn a horse stomped. Over on the boulevard a car honked.

"What's it honking for this time of the night?" Birdeen asked.

"Go to bed, Mama," I said. "You're tired."

"I'm dog-tired," Birdeen admitted. "The whole Civil War's too much for one woman—on top of everything else."

"I'll fix things for breakfast."

"I'm willing. I can't hold my head up any longer."

I followed my mother into the kitchen. The stair to the bedrooms opened out of the kitchen.

"Mama," I said.

"Say it, say it," my mother urged, "don't keep me waiting."

I wasn't sure I could say it.

"Ask Papa not to sing 'Sweet Marie' so loud when he gets up in the morning."

My mother, lifting her skirt preparatory to climbing, answered, "I will. I've been meaning to. That song's beginning to get on my nerves, too."

Birdeen closed the door behind her, and, left alone, I felt a mixture of loneliness and command, like a captain on an abandoned ship. Birdeen's contest costume glimmered in the living room like the ghost of a woman. Reno's big ranch hat hung on the back of his chair, where he had tossed it when he came in, after carrying the last of the tomatoes to the porch. The night wind rising set the barn door to creaking. I stood firmly planted in the middle of the kitchen floor. Even so weighted, it seemed to me, the room, the house, the ranch, all might disappear, carrying me into the night's unknown darkness.

4

I stayed on in the dark sitting room after Birdeen went upstairs to bed. Parents, with their hard work and bills and differences of opinion, need so much more sleep than children. They are worn out with worrying and disagreeing. Except for Mama's performance tomorrow, I didn't have a worry in the world. Being switched on the legs with a milkweed stalk, especially since it had been endured in order to spare another, was nothing to fret about. The present hour was fine, and being saved took care of eternity.

I let the light burn on in the kitchen though it was a waste of coal oil. I liked the idea of being unseen and seeing. Until Zen came in, nothing caught my eyes except the coffeepot ready to go for breakfast and Birdeen's curling iron, which didn't stir my imagination very much.

Zen did. As one of the family, he came in without knocking, calling out as usual, "Heigh-ho, everybody."

"Shh," I said. "Everybody's asleep."

Zen stopped in his tracks, then hung his coat carefully on the back of a kitchen chair and loosened the knot of his tie. A widower of thirty, Zen had been, in my father's words, out sparking. Courting was what my mother called what a McManus did when he stepped a girl out. I, who knew more about Zen's habits than either my father or my mother, didn't know what to call it.

Zen had on a lavender pin-striped shirt. This was the

color I thought you would get if you mixed the purple-black of Zen's hair with the blue of his eyes.

"Hi, Aunt Jetty," he said.

"Hi," I answered.

I had been Aunt Jetty to Zen for so long that any other name coming from him would seem strange.

It had started back East when I was only four years old. Reno had brought me up to Grandma's house because Birdeen was having a little brother at our own home. Of course, until Neddie came, no one knew that the baby would be a little brother. But big sisters always went away from home when there was a baby being born.

It had been a snowy night, and my father had dumped me at Grandma's door without even going in to say hello or warm himself. Grandma was with Birdeen, and Grandpa was feeding the stock. I was alone in the parlor except for a man I had never seen before. The stranger was sitting in front of the grate with his long thin legs stretched out toward the fire. He didn't get up when Reno closed the front door, but he did turn in his chair to see who had arrived.

"Well, if it isn't Aunt Jetty."

I knew then who he was: my uncle Zen, home from California, where he had gone for his health. He had sent me postcards of big trees and ostrich farms, addressed to "Aunt Jetty."

How could a niece be an aunt to an uncle, I wondered —and asked him.

"I call you Aunt Jetty because you are a born aunt."

"How can you tell?"

"By looking at you."

"You just saw me."

"I saw you when you were a baby. It don't take long to find out a thing like that."

"Are you a born uncle?"

"Nope. Your mother made me an uncle. There are a lot of things she wanted to make me and failed. But she made me an uncle, all right."

"Did she make me an aunt?"

"I told you. You were born an aunt. But your mother probably had a hand in seeing you stayed that way."

I didn't know whether being born an aunt was good or bad. I didn't know what Zen thought about aunts. I felt somehow belittled by the word "aunt." I had remained on the threshold of the room, hood and coat still on; the thin long-legged man still sat unmoving before the fire.

"Don't you want to be an aunt?"

I knew it didn't seem right for me to be my uncle Zen's aunt. Still, it seemed rude to refuse a name he had given me.

"I need an aunt," Zen had wheedled. "I don't have any."

Still I said nothing.

Then Zen had asked, "How would you like to be my little sweetheart?"

He said that in a different voice. I knew even then the difference between sweethearts and aunts and knew that men spoke of them in different ways. The minute I heard the sweetheart invitation, I had felt free to take off my coat and hood and join Zen at the fire.

His coat off, tie loosened, Zen remained in the kitchen doorway.

"First time you ever heard that name, Aunt, you didn't like it."

"That was a long time ago."

"Eight years," Zen said. Still standing in the doorway between kitchen and sitting room and still looking at me, he said, "I'd swear it was twelve."

"That would make me sixteen."

"That's exactly what I meant. You're a Chalmers, for looks. They're all early bloomers."

"Mama says I don't have a drop of Chalmers blood in me."

"I don't see how she managed that."

"She couldn't change my looks, of course, but she could make me act like a McManus."

"She's done that, all right. And I ought to know, being a McManus myself. What's going on here? Somebody get sleepy before they got upstairs and began undressing?"

"It's Mama's clothes for the contest tomorrow night."

"Contest?"

"The W.C.T.U. contest against liquor."

"What's your mama going to do?"

"Speak a piece."

"Against liquor?"

"Of course she's against liquor, but her piece is about Kentucky Belle."

"That's a winner, liquor or no liquor."

Zen took a bottle from his pocket, a liquor bottle, I could tell from its shape, and took three good long swallows. "Here's to Kentucky Belle," he said.

"I shouldn't be sitting talking to a drinker."

"Maybe you could reform me."

"Mama's tried and she didn't."

"Aunts have more power than sisters—sometimes."

"Uncle Zen, did you ever hear of anyone getting gin in their nose?"

"Nope. Never did. Where'd you hear of that?"

"Mrs. Ashton. She's going to speak a piece about someone who got gin in his nose and became a drunkard."

"Marie Ashton, eh? That don't strike me as being a very sensible way of getting drunk."

"It's the same as getting a taste for something, she says. Just the smell is enough to make you want another drink."

"She going to recite tomorrow night?"

"Yes, she is. She'll be Mama's biggest rival."

"I reckon I better be there. Cheer your mother on."

"She won't be cheered to have her brother at a temperance meeting with liquor in his pocket."

"I don't know what your mother would do without you, Aunt Jetty. I'll leave the liquor home. How about a game of Seven Up?"

"We don't have any cards in the house. You know that."

"I know that." Zen took a pack of playing cards from his pocket.

"We could play Rook."

"I don't know how to play Rook and you know how to play Seven Up. I taught you."

"We mustn't disturb Mama. She needs her rest."

"We won't disturb her."

Zen shuffled the cards so that a stream of them hung together between his two hands as if threaded on a string. He looked like the pictures of Robert Louis Stevenson. What Robert Louis Stevenson really looked like was a long, lean, lank-haired gambling man.

Zen drank and wasn't a drunkard; played cards and wasn't a gambler. What he did was sell automobiles and make money. But with the cards in his hands and the liquor in his pocket, he not only looked like a riverboat gambler, but he was acting like one, too.

Gambling and liquor were no temptation to me. Whiskey tasted nasty. I'd been given a teaspoonful after a dose of castor oil. Gambling was chance-taking, and what I liked was a sure thing. Even before I was saved, I knew that some acts that were harmless to one person should be avoided because they might tempt an onlooker and be his downfall. Zen, already a drinker and card player, couldn't be harmed by my playing. Better with me than with some crony who might cheat, get drunk, and fight. I might even be saving Zen's life.

I took the ornaments off the stand table and put it between our two chairs.

"Cut for deal," said Zen.

I cut high.

"Never play cards with a lucky woman," said Zen.

"Is it worse to play with a lucky woman than a lucky man?"

"Much worse."

"How could that be? People are people. Luck's luck."

"You missed one point. Men aren't women."

"What difference does that make?"

"You can stop playing with a man who's lucky. You maybe won't want to stop with a woman."

"Even when you're losing?"

"Yeh. You'd rather lose with her than not be with her at all."

"Not Neddie. He stops playing the minute he starts losing. He doesn't like to play with me even when he wins."

"Neddie's a very strange card player."

"He thinks I'm bossy."

"What do you think?"

"I do it for his own good."

"Well, you're just his sister, not his Aunt Jetty."

Zen, though he wasn't a small or dainty man, played cards the way a hummingbird eats: quick delicate motions, no thump or thud on the table as he played a card. I liked the flick and dart of his long-fingered brown hands as he laid out the cards. The skin between his fingers was white like the band at the top of his forehead that his hat covered.

Seven Up, even though we weren't gambling, was more exciting than Rook because it was wrong. This was an unfair advantage the devil had. Seven Up was not a whit more interesting than Rook except for its bad name. Gamblers and drinkers and gunslingers played it; this knowledge, plus the fact that the man across the table from me had a bottle in his pocket, made me tremble with excitement. I was lucky at cards, but so was Zen, and he was also more experienced. He treated me like a real opponent, though; not a kid whose feelings had to be protected. He skunked me three times, then said, "How about a little refreshment?"

I was afraid he meant liquor, but what he had in mind was coffee.

"Coffeepot's all set to go, I see."

He lit a burner of the Florence coal-oil stove and put the pot on.

"How about you, Aunt Jetty?"

"No, thanks." Coffee tasted brackish to me. But I knew that grownups, as they got older, needed pills and liniments, coffee and liquor to keep them going.

When Zen returned with a big mug of coffee and a handful of Birdeen's gingersnaps, I asked him a question I had often thought about.

"Did you want to be nicknamed Zen because you were ashamed of being called Zenith?"

"Nothing shameful about being Zenith."

"It means the highest and best. Like Apex or Acme. I'd hate it. It must seem pretty biggity to other people, calling yourself the highest and best."

Zen laughed so hard he sprayed cookie crumbs onto the playing cards. He cleaned them with his handkerchief.

"What makes you think I named myself?"

"You haven't stopped it."

"Back where I come from, and you, too, it didn't seem biggity. My mother named me Zenith because I was born in the town of Zenith, Indiana."

"I didn't know people got named for towns."

"Trees, towns, flowers, states. There's a Missouri Overturff lives not ten miles from here. I sold a car to a Golden West just last week."

"There's no state named Golden West."

"That's what some people call California. I was pretty lucky being born in Zenith. I might've been born in the town of Gnaw Bone. How'd you like an Uncle Gnaw Bone? All bone until recently, and no gnaw. Or Bean Blossom? Have to be Uncle Bean, because I'm no blossom. There's a town called Stony Lonesome, too."

I laughed. What could he do with a name like that?

Zen didn't try to make an uncle out of Stony Lonesome. "I'm glad I missed Stony Lonesome, though. That's a state—a state of mind, that is—I've been through a few times and I don't like it. It's my plan to give it a miss."

"I know why I'm an aunt. Why am I Jetty?"

"My God," said Zen, "I reckoned you'd figured that out the first time you looked in a mirror."

"You shouldn't take the name of the Lord in vain, Uncle Zen," I said.

"I forgot you were saved last week."

"Saved or unsaved, it's wrong."

"Why?"

"It's a cussword used the way you said it."

"God'll forgive me. How about you, Aunt Jetty?"

Cussing couldn't harm me, so I had nothing to forgive. It was the cusser who was in trouble. Zen could figure this out for himself.

"If you'd looked in the mirror and seen those jet

black eyes and that jet black hair, you'd have known why you were 'Aunt Jetty.' It's the Chalmers in you."

"Is jet black good?"

"I couldn't think of a prettier color, Aunt Jetty."

Birdeen, who had come down the back stairs from the bedroom, stood in the door to the kitchen.

"Ginerva, what are you doing up at this hour?"

Zen answered for me. "Making a visitor feel at home, Birdeen."

"Zen, you don't need a schoolgirl to make you feel at home here. Playing cards and drinking—"

"This is coffee I'm drinking."

"Don't think I can't smell. You may be sobering up on coffee, Zen, but there was liquor before the coffee."

Zen took the bottle out of his pocket and thumped it down on the table.

"You got a nose for liquor, Birdeen."

"Don't you joke about such things. Drinking, playing cards, telling a schoolgirl she's pretty. Ginerva, you get right upstairs. You know what a big day we have tomorrow. Rest and sleep is what we need, not talk. Zen, you take your saloon stuff on to some place where it's more welcome than here."

I scurried toward the stairs without a word.

"Good night, Aunt Jetty," Zen called after me.

Mama, pale as an unlit candle in her long unbleached-muslin nightgown, sank onto the chair I had vacated. Zen half filled his empty coffee cup from the bottle.

"Zen, you shouldn't go putting ideas in Ginerva's head."

"What are heads for?"

"You know what I mean. Telling her she's pretty."

"What I said was the color of her hair and eyes was pretty. What's the harm in that? Ginerva's kept so busy with school and housework and minding the kids and getting saved on the side, she'll end up a Cinderella falling for the first fellow who gives her a kiss. And it's only in fairy tales that the first kisser turns out to be a Prince Charming. She'd better have a little praise here at home so she won't be so carried away the first time she hears it from someone else."

"That wasn't the way I was brought up."

"Me neither, Sis. And look at us."

"I'm trying so hard."

Birdeen cradled her head in her arms on the table. I watched from the stairway. "I haven't been able to sleep," she said.

Zen might have liked to have said, "This'll help," and hand her what remained in his coffee cup. He'd get the contents back in his face, like enough, which wouldn't hurt him, but would fill Birdeen with so much remorse she wouldn't be able to sleep for weeks.

The truth was, she tried too hard, harder than anyone who weighed only ninety-eight pounds could endure. She'd never find a better husband than Reno, but because he was a member of a ne'er-do-well family, she was bound and determined by her actions alone, if necessary, to teach him better ways.

She might have had the strength for that if there hadn't been in her, too, some urge—I wasn't sure how to name it—to mount a platform and speak her piece. So there she was, pulled two ways at once and not enough of her to make it one way easily, let alone two.

As a dealer in cars, Zen knew more about their mechanism than he did about his sister's nature. Birdeen was a neat little four-cylinder roadster, never built for heavy-duty work or brutal race-track competition. She had had her mind set on both: pick the tomatoes and give Marie Ashton a run for her money in a temperance race. Maybe stop Zen from drinking, too, even if she couldn't protect Ginerva from discovering that she was a pretty girl and steer Neddie clear of words like "belly button," "butt," and "puke."

"Poor kid."

He probably hadn't intended to speak aloud, but his whisper half roused his sleeping sister.

"Zen? Are you drinking?"

"No, thinking."

"We had such great hopes for you, Zen."

"I know you did."

Birdeen dropped her head back onto the cradle of her arm.

"Don't wake me up, Zen."

Zen poured his next drink into his cup very quietly. The cards might have been snowflakes, they drifted into their box so quietly. It was Reno's presence, not any sound he made, that caused Zen to turn in his chair. Reno tiptoed into the room.

"She asleep?" Reno asked.

Zen nodded.

"She ought to be in bed."

"She ought."

"She can't sleep there all night. She'll have a crick in her neck so she can't recite."

"Carry her up."

"It'll make her mad."

"I reckon you've seen that before. Can't you put a stop to this tomato picking?"

"How?"

"Why's she doing it?"

"Proving how work-brickle the McManuses are."

"Oh, God," Zen said. "Too bad I didn't get tarred with that brush."

Reno went over to Birdeen, lifted her like a baby, and Birdeen, babylike, leaned in close to his shoulder without opening her eyes.

"Take me to bed, Reno. It's late."

Zen turned back to the table and his bottle. He put it in his pocket, thought better of that, took it out, poured himself another, then sat drinking slowly.

5

I didn't come downstairs in my nightgown as Birdeen had done. Zen was no brother of mine. I had slipped out of my nightgown and into my cover-all school apron. I threw my arms around Zen's neck and whispered, "Mama didn't mean that, Uncle Zen. She's upset because of the contest. You know she doesn't want you staying away from here."

Zen hugged me. "I know it, Aunt Jetty. But you were sweet to come down and tell me. Just sit with me 'til I finish this drink and I'll be on my way. I've got work to do tomorrow, too. You and I've been through some hard times together. This is pinhead stuff compared with what's past."

The conversation of two people remembering, if the memory is enjoyable to both, rocks on like music or love-making. There is a rhythm and a predictability to it that each anticipates and relishes. The note sounded requires the one that follows: so stroke on stroke and sound on sound, the edifice is built of harmony or desire in the remembered past.

For a little girl, an uncle is so much more of a man than a father. Or perhaps it was only the difference between Zen and Reno. And of course Birdeen. Birdeen had tamed Reno as she had never been able to tame her brother. Are all fathers, if well tamed, nothing more than awkward mothers? Persons with divided skirts who, inside the house, and that's where the little girl sees him, are so much less deft and capable than the mother? The uncle isn't diminished in that way. He doesn't attempt, not before the little girl anyway, what he isn't good at. Perhaps this is the way it should be. I had never been my father's little sweetheart. Mama had never presented Reno to me in that way—as a man of enigmatic charm, deeply loved, and also deeply mistrusted. Birdeen's trust in Reno reduced him for me. The childish imagination takes fire at the merest hint of unknown evil, and remains sluggish in the face of demonstrated virtue. Zen was unknown evil.

The night when I was four, Uncle Zen had taken me upon his knee. He had warmed me at the fire, rocked me, and talked to me. He was lonesome that night, newly home, newly recovered from a long sickness. His mother was away; his father, who disapproved of him, was keeping himself busy in the barn. His sister, to whom he might have confided, was busy having a baby. And Zen was in love and separated from his love. Because of his love, he was drawn to, and tender and magnanimous toward, everyone at that time. Love is like the measles. It's catching. People who are in love are dusted with love germs like pollen. Zen had not only love germs, but also a fund of physical tenderness that he needed to expend—but which not everyone wanted. He couldn't be fondling and nuzzling strangers; he couldn't blow gently into his father's ear; or nibble the points of his mother's fingers.

That left me. He saw me as "Aunt Jetty," but he needed a "little sweetheart" even more, to take, temporarily, "big sweetheart's" place. Becoming a little sweetheart at four was a transfiguring experience for me. I was never out of Zen's arms for long. He carried me, no light load, from room to room. Grandpa scolded him.

"That child will lose the use of her legs if you don't put her down soon." Or "You'll have another breakdown if you don't stop lugging that big girl around."

Zen wasn't the kind of man to be held back by anyone's disapproval, let alone his father's.

"Aunt Jetty's light as a feather," he said. Then he blew in my ear and carried me upstairs to his slant-roofed room, where we reclined on his bed and he taught me to play Seven Up. First a little sweetheart, then a gambler! At four, I felt that I had plumbed life's depths. But this was as nothing compared with what was to come. I met the "big sweetheart."

I didn't know then what was keeping Zen from his big sweetheart. I knew that my grandparents disapproved of Love Lewis. Love's parents were renters, which meant to Zen's parents that they were lazy and shiftless. Maybe the Lewises didn't approve of Zen. All a girl needed to do, Birdeen said, was to go out with Zen a couple of times to get a bad name. Once wouldn't do it. The girl might not know Zen's reputation. But after the first night she knew it, and if she went out the second time, she was supposed to be willing.

Whatever the reasons for Zen's not seeing Love Lewis were, their separation, by his stay in California, hadn't taken her out of his mind. On the fourth day after my arrival, he asked me to take a belated Christmas gift to Love Lewis.

I went because I wanted to please Zen, but my heart shrank when he asked me to go. So long as Love Lewis was someone Zen was never going to see again, I could hear about her as if she were a girl in a fairy tale. Now, though I was still "little sweetheart," I knew that it wasn't actually a question of size, of big or little, but of "first" and "second." I was second. Or perhaps not even second. Perhaps wholly "Aunt Jetty" now. I thought sullenly about saying "No," but I reasoned myself into going. Love Lewis might be first, but when I got back from delivering the present, who'd be *with* Zen? I would. Who'd talk about it? We would. Who'd be on Zen's knee, cheeks burning from the caress of his black-stubbled face? I would. What did titles matter? Big, little, first, second? Zen knew how to train a girl to be the other woman—and how to make her like it.

To deliver the present, Uncle Zen asked me to stay off the road and to cut through the woods, where I would be less liable to be seen.

It wasn't a long walk, but on a dark winter afternoon it was a scary one. In that neighborhood, even children knew that "bad things" happened in the woods, things worse for children because they didn't know what the "bad things" were. I tried to reassure myself before I started by telling myself that I was going to take a walk "through the trees." Trees didn't frighten me; but to call the woods trees was not much more helpful than calling a man who is threatening you nothing but arms and legs. In the woods there was a presence dark and threatening that a thousand trees could not account for.

I never told Zen my fears; not to save him worry, but out of pride. I didn't want him to know how much I was willing to suffer in order to continue in his favor.

I met Love at the other side of the woods. Zen's girls always had names like that. He never went with a Mildred Suggs or a Sadie Banks or even a Louise Walters. Zen didn't pick Love for her name, of course, but he was the kind of a man who gravitated toward such names and toward girls who looked like Love Lewis.

There were patches of snow still unmelted in the shade of the trees. Love was outside walking slowly along the snake fence that separated the Lewis farm from the woods. She had on a housedress of pink flowered percale and a knitted or crocheted shawl of black pulled tight around her shoulders and tucked in under her crossed forearms. She had dark hair and eyes, high cheekbones, and a square face set on a slender neck. She looked like a princess to me.

Before I went home to my new little brother, Love Lewis was my friend. I told her what I hadn't told Zen, how frightened I was of the trip through the woods. Love sympathized with me, but she never said, "This is too much to ask of a four-year-old. You mustn't come again." Instead, she hugged and kissed me, rocked me in her arms, and called me a "brave baby."

I was hugged and kissed at each end of the trip, but never for myself. I was the go-between. I received second-hand kisses and proxy hugs. I was Zen to Love, and Love to Zen. I was seized upon, smothered with kisses, questioned and praised by both. I had power with each, saw it, and used it. With Love, I imitated Zen, was manly and swaggering. With Zen, I was Love, small and flushed and listening. I lost sight of who I was. I was just somebody's loving armful.

Love Lewis died in April of the same sickness that had sent Zen to California. Grandma wrote Birdeen the news and asked if I could come for a visit. Zen had suffered a setback himself, and he had been much taken with me when I was there. He often spoke of Aunt Jetty, and my grandmother was sure the child was just the distraction he needed to rouse him up and get him interested in life again.

Zen's reaction to the death of a sweetheart was exactly, in my opinion, what it should be. The least a man could do when his sweetheart died was to have a breakdown. Zen's parents didn't grieve much because of Love's death. It was untimely and unfortunate, of course, for Love, but it was a blessing for Zen. He'd mourn her for a while, naturally, then he'd settle on someone more suitable.

Either because he was truly sick, or because he was heartsick, or both, Zen spent his days in his bay-windowed upstairs room. A Juneberry tree was busy unfolding its damp deep-veined leaves almost inside his room. The windmill whirled and creaked in the gusty April weather. Shadows of leaves and shadows of windmill blades when the sun shone, cloud shadows when it didn't, filled the room with motion as well as dark and light. The creak of the windmill, the motion of the leaves, the surflike wash of light and shadow made Zen's room seem like a lighthouse to me, or a ship itself.

There was no more Seven Up. Zen tried, but he didn't care in the least who won. If he didn't care, I didn't care, and the whole point of a game is wanting to win.

There was no more talk of "big sweetheart," "little sweetheart." No secret departures, surreptitious returns, whispered accounts of how she had looked and what she had said.

Instead, Zen decided, as a heartbroken but still active man might decide to break a colt, to teach me how to read. There was no question of "reading readiness." Zen was full of "teaching readiness." I was going to learn to read, ready or not. I was not averse to learning to read, but I was nothing like as eager to learn as Zen was to teach.

There was a touch of sadism in the energy with which Zen taught. Perhaps it eased his pain to see someone else suffer. I cried a good deal, but I didn't blame him. I blamed myself for being so slow and for causing Zen so much trouble. I liked him—admired and worshiped him, really—for being so strong and relentless.

At the end of my visit I could read, and not baby stuff like "The cat is on the mat." The textbook Zen used was a book of African travels. I was surer of big words, such as "python," "gorilla," "crocodile," and "Swahili," than I was of little easy words like "was" and "saw," "go" and "got," "am" and "is."

The big peculiar words stuck in my mind, though I never knew exactly what the crocodile was up to. Was-ing or saw-ing? Going or getting? Eating or tearing? Zen's teaching upset my entire educational timing. When other kids were reading *The Sunbonnet Girls* and *The Overall Boys,* I was reading *The Trail of the Lonesome Pine* and *The Clansmen.*

Sometimes Zen stopped teaching to do a strange thing. The peculiar act was possible because of a peculiar choice he had made, one I was never able to understand. Why had he chosen Love Lewis's glasses? For that's what he had done. Offered after her death a keepsake by her parents, Zen had chosen her glasses. Love's glasses were the rimless kind, and with Love's dark eyes and brows they were, if not invisible, certainly not noticeable. But why glasses? Why not a lock of her hair or a favorite book or a breast pin? That choice, so unromantic, offended my image of Zen as a romantic and dashing fellow. But if this choice was puzzling, what he did with them in the midst of a reading lesson was more puzzling still.

Suddenly interrupting a paragraph where a crocodile was eating, Zen would snatch those spectacles from the pocket where he kept them and slap them in a great hurry onto his face. Then he would sit silent, unmoving, gazing out into the leafy-rustle windmill-clatter sun-and-shadow April world. Silent and staring for a long time, it seemed to me.

When he put on Love's spectacles, did he see something that was hidden to me? Perhaps they were very strong and, with them on, he could see the bug a bird in the Juneberry tree was eating. Perhaps, since they hadn't been made for him, they pulled the world outside the window into the shape he imagined Love had seen. Perhaps it was the feel of the glasses on his face he liked.

71

Perhaps it was like having Love herself touch him. Whatever it was, he remained silent and staring. For how long? A half hour?

I longed to try on the glasses. Or even to ask Zen, "What do you see?" I was too proud or too cowardly to ask. Besides, Zen was my world. I could look at him.

Then, as suddenly as he had put the glasses on, he would snatch them off, whip them back into his pocket, and, pointing his finger at a word, demand, as if I had been causing the delay, "What is that?"

"Rhinocerous," I would shout, too loud and too pleased with Zen's return to be able to control my voice.

"I'm not deaf, Aunt Jetty," Zen would say and would point to another word.

"Zebra," I would whisper.

Deception and dead sweethearts and frightening trips through dark wintry woods and learning, even fiercely forced, these are enigmatic keepsakes.

Yet, that night, even with Birdeen overworked and overwrought, with the contest coming tomorrow, with bad dreams, and Marie Ashton poking Reno with her parasol, Zen was right about present life. It was all pinhead stuff compared with the past.

What we remembered was long ago, back East, in another country; the pain almost forgotten, the good remembered. Zen, since then, had buried one wife and divorced another. He still carried Love Lewis's spectacles with him, but he spoke of her now as he might of a woman in a book.

There was cause for pride in our memories. We had survived. I had made those frightening trips, had learned those enormous words. I had received those hugs and kisses, had been called "brave baby" and "little sweetheart."

And it hadn't really stopped, though the words had changed. That very night I had been told that jet black was pretty, that I took after the Chalmerses, who were the lookers, that I could easily be taken for a sixteen-year-old.

Zen poured the last tablespoons of the whiskey into his coffee cup, drank them down, held the bottle up and said, "I reckon your mama wouldn't like this left on the place."

"I could bury it," I said.

"Might sprout a whiskey tree."

"Bottles don't grow."

"Trust Aunt Jetty to know the answers."

I felt rebuked. Reprimanded for being a know-it-all.

"That's right, Aunt Jetty. I'm counting on your knowing all the answers. It's not been my long suit."

Zen put the empty bottle in his pocket. "Time for me to clear out. Your mother's got enough to worry about without my adding a drunken brother to the lot."

I bounced to my feet even before Zen. "You're no more drunk than I am, Uncle Zen."

"That might be," Zen said.

After he put on his coat, he took the spectacles from his pocket. I thought that he would put them on. Instead, he looked at them, not through them. After a minute or two of inspection, he handed the spectacles to me.

"Put these on, Ginerva," he said.

I had often wanted to do that, to see the world Zen saw. There was no change. The same slab-sided man, thin and dark, I had always seen stood in front of me.

But Zen must have seen someone else. "Love," he said, and clasped me to him. He kissed me and hugged me as he hadn't been able when I was his little sweetheart. I was almost his height now and could be kissed without standing on my toes at all.

He took the glasses from me quickly. Then, with bottle, playing cards, and Love's spectacles in his pocket, he went to the door.

"See you tomorrow night at the contest," he said.

I waited until I could no longer hear his automobile before I turned out the light and went upstairs.

6

Uncle Zen had a part in the contest. Not a part he wanted or that did the cause of temperance any good, but we talked about it long and often.

Uncle Zen was selling Hupmobiles that day as usual, I suppose. Birdeen was picking tomatoes. I was keeping the house neat and had Neddie's and Ramona's clothes laid out ready for them to put on.

The church where the contest was going to take place was only a step down the road from our place. Already the W.C.T.U. ladies were arriving. With their husbands as helpers, they were carrying palm fronds, smilax, strands of bougainvillaea, and armloads of geraniums and Shasta daisies into the church.

So many flowers and the white dresses for purity, which the temperance ladies always wore on official occasions, made me feel as if I were going to a wedding.

I left the window and examined the clothes Neddie and Ramona were to wear. The September evening was warm, and there was no need to get them trussed up in their Sunday best until about seven-fifteen. The program began at seven-thirty; it was now six-twenty.

I took a last look at myself in the mirror of the bird's-eye maple dresser before I went downstairs. I was dressed for the occasion. My back-East grandmother had sent me a lavender Soiesette dress. With it I wore a white dimity guimpe, electric-blue hair ribbons, long white cotton stockings, and a new pair of black patent-leather Mary Janes. I didn't think I was pretty, but I did think I was well turned out. Earlier in the day, I had worn a buttermilk mask to bleach my freckles. It had bleached them, all right, from brown to pink, which wasn't much of an improvement.

In their separate ways, my mother and father had tried to reassure me about the color change.

"They'll never be seen from a galloping horse," Birdeen said.

Reno, killing two birds with one stone, complimenting Birdeen and cheering me up, said, "Your mother's the only one people will have eyes for this evening."

It was because of Birdeen that the pink freckles worried me. I wanted to be a credit to her. I worried about my mother most of the time, but tonight, with Birdeen reciting, I didn't want my worry to show. I went down the stairs, somberly, but when I reached the kitchen, where Birdeen was curling her hair, I began to whistle loudly and cheerfully.

"Do you have to be so noisy, Ginerva?"

"I was tiptoeing."

"That's the trouble. If you're going to whistle like that, come in stomping so I'll have some warning." In her embroidered corset cover and her petticoat with lace-edged ruffles, Birdeen looked like a society lady dressed for a ball. It was too bad, I thought, that she couldn't recite her piece that way.

"What do you want, anyway?" Birdeen asked.

I didn't want a thing. I was in the kitchen because I couldn't help myself. Birdeen drew me like a magnet—

not that I always wanted to be drawn. Sometimes I hated my mother, who wasn't the fairest or most logical woman in the world. Yelling at me just now, when I had taken care of the house and the kids all day so she could pick the tomatoes she had been determined, for some reason, to pick. On this day, of all days. I excused her now because of the strain of the contest. Birdeen took the curling iron from the lamp chimney, tested it with spit, and waved it through the air to cool it.

I thought of a reason for being in the kitchen.

"Mama, I know your recitation by heart. If you feel yourself stumbling, just look at me. I'll be saying the word you need."

Birdeen turned away from the mirror over the sink, arms upraised, curl smoking a little.

"I don't intend to stumble, Ginerva."

Birdeen said this like a fact. She unwound a brown, singed curl. She reheated the iron. Her arms lifted and fell, her hands turned and turned. Half of her forehead was covered with ringlets. The lamp, in the September dusk, made a curious circle of yellow light. There was a smell of coal oil and burned hair in the room. The boxes of tomatoes on the back porch smelled like a field. A mockingbird sang in the pepper tree. Under the tree, playing house, Neddie and Ramona were having a quiet husband-and-wife argument. The palm tree creaked in the evening air.

Reno came onto the back porch with a box of tomatoes, dirty and mad. He banged the box down. "There you are, Birdeen. There's the last box. I hope to goodness you're satisfied."

"I'm sorry to have put you to all the trouble of carrying them here, Reno."

"Don't waste any pity on me."

"Get cleaned up, then. We're due at the church in less than an hour."

"I don't care whether I go or not. See you standing up there worn out from picking tomatoes all day, before you ever start reciting."

"I can do whatever has to be done."

"Come right down to it, neither one *has* to be done. Pick tomatoes *or* recite."

"I promised the W.C.T.U. two months ago."

"Why didn't you give up tomato picking, then?"

"You know why, Reno Chalmers."

"No, I don't. Unless you're hunting for an excuse to blame me in case you lose."

"Don't say that," I ordered my father. "Don't think it. Mama will win. Marie Ashton hasn't a chance."

"Who said anything about Marie Ashton?" my father asked.

"It's between her and Mama. You know that," I said meaningfully.

Reno grabbed my arm. "Ginerva—" he began.

"Let her alone," Birdeen told him. "She didn't do anything but say I'd win. That's no crime, is it?"

"Maybe he doesn't want you to win," I suggested.

Before Birdeen could reply to that, Reno took my arm and waltzed me outside so fast my Mary Janes only touched earth now and then.

"Now, young lady," he asked when he had me in the back yard, "what was the meaning of that?"

"I had a bad dream about you and Marie Ashton."

"What do you mean, 'bad dream'?"

"I dreamed that she was in the choir and that you stood up in church and sang 'Sweet Marie' to her."

"She isn't even in the choir," Reno said.

"In my dream, she was. You stood up and sang,

" 'In the morn when I awake,
     Sweet Marie,
   Seems to me my heart will break,
     Love, for thee.' "

Reno gave a big snort, filled the washbasin at the hydrant, put it on the wash bench, and took off his shirt.

"The trouble with you and your mother is that both of you've got more imagination than you know what to do with."

"Did Mama dream it, too?"

Papa unbuttoned his B.V.D. top and let it hang around his belt.

"She's got more sense than that, anyway."

"You sing 'Sweet Marie' all the time."

"Aren't you worried about me and Annie Laurie? And darling Nellie Gray? And Nita Juanita?"

"They don't live here."

Reno, blowing soap bubbles, and not stopping his lathering, said, "If I had time for it, Ginerva, I'd give you a good sound switching right here and now."

"I can't help what I dream."

"You can help talking about it when it's ugly."

"You want me to be quiet about it?"

79

I thought maybe Reno was going to make time for the switching.

"Who do you think you are, anyway?" he asked. "Some kind of a lawyer with a criminal on trial?"

All I wanted him to do was say, "I love Birdeen with all my heart and soul." But how could I ask my own father that?

"Who do you want to win the contest?" I asked. "Really and truly?"

Reno picked up his washbasin of water, and for a second I thought he was going to throw it at me. Instead, he let it dribble onto the ground like a man without strength.

"Ginerva," he said solemnly, "it's a wonder to goodness your mother don't have a worse case of the heebie-jeebies than she's got, with you underfoot all day. Now, you listen to me. I don't want to hear another word out of you. You take Ramona and Neddie over to the church, and the three of you sit there and don't make a move or a sound 'til I get there. You got that straight?"

I nodded.

Then, "See that you do it," he said.

"Look straight ahead," I commanded Neddie and Ramona as I led them into the church. I had the idea that as children of a contestant, in our best clothes (and I so recently saved in that very building), our entrance would be noticed, of importance to all. Under these circumstances, I wanted our bearing to be modest. I wanted us to walk in as if we were just anybody, unsaved, wearing old clothes, and not connected with the program in any way. It wasn't easy for me to pretend any of this. I could feel my heart beating in my cheeks and fingertips. Without the facts that set us apart, I was excited by the crowd and the prospect of an evening's entertainment, which was also a contest. And there was an added fact, of which I alone was aware: my mother would be contending with a rival for her husband's love.

In spite of our good clothes and relationship to a contestant, we might have been on our way to prayer meeting on any Wednesday night—until Zen joined us. Then we were noticed. There was nothing about Zen's appearance to suggest that he had ever had a bottle in his pocket or a playing card in his hand. He looked like what he was: a well-to-do young businessman, one who had had the foresight to get into the car-selling business while the poor ranchers were still waiting for their orange groves to come into full bearing. If he had had a wife, she wouldn't have to be picking tomatoes in order to pay the bills. Zen had other men's wives at work to help meet the payments on the new Hupmobile their husbands' oranges wouldn't pay for.

"Hi, kiddo," Uncle Zen said. He was talking to me, not Ramona or Neddie. He would have called them kids. "Kiddo" was a girl, not a kid. He took me by the arm as if we had come together, as if we were a couple. There wasn't any liquor smell on him this evening. Shaving lotion, maybe, something almost as sweet as Birdeen's Florida Water.

With Zen with us, there was no longer any point in trying to act like one of the crowd. Everyone knew Zen. He was Zenith McManus, the most successful automobile dealer in Orange County; the contest took on tone the minute he parked his coupe at the hitching rack beside the outmoded Dobbins and Dollies.

"Mama didn't expect you," I said.

"Why not? She's my sister."

"The subject matter," I explained patiently.

"Temperance? I'm a hundred percent for temperance. A drunk with a horse is at least as smart as his horse. A drunk with a car had as well start down the pike taking target practice at passers-by. Let's go find a seat. Looks like an S.R.O. crowd."

"What's that mean?" asked Neddie.

"No place to sit."

"Standing room only," I, accustomed to keeping Neddie on the right track, said.

"I thought I'd maybe lost Aunt Jetty," Zen said, "but I see she's still with us."

Very little had needed to be done to make the church suitable for an elocution contest. Only the pulpit had to be carried out. Except for it and two small blackboards, one announcing attendance and collection, and the other hymn numbers, the church was like any small bare hall designed for speechmaking. I was sorry the blackboards had been left. They took away from the magic that the temperance ladies had been able to work on that bare brown platform. It no longer looked like the place where I had been saved; or where anyone *could* be saved. It was a green cave, dripping with smilax, studded with brilliant flowers and walled with palm fronds and pepper boughs. Ten empty chairs awaited those who would perform there.

It was almost, I imagined, like a real theater. The temperance ladies had typewritten programs with the names of each contestant, her selection, and the rules of the contest. The rules provided that speakers would be judged on a scale of twenty percent for appearance, twenty percent for selection, and sixty percent for delivery. Appearance didn't mean whether you were pretty or not, though everyone agreed that no contestant was going to be hurt by being good-looking and wearing a knockout dress. But what the Christian Temperance Union meant by appearance, at least at an elocution contest, was how you held yourself on the platform: your gestures, demeanor, or sobriety and grace. I thought Birdeen would score as well as anyone in appearance. She wasn't actually as pretty as Marie Ashton; and Mrs. Ashton's dress wouldn't be homemade. But if the rules meant what they said, Birdeen could gesture circles around Marie Ashton, and outdemeanor her six ways to sunset.

The real trouble was Birdeen's selection. If it was true that the judges were going to favor recitations having to do with drunkenness, because this was a temperance program, Birdeen was sunk. I longed to have a personal word with each of the judges. I would tell them: " 'Kentucky Belle' teaches people to be brave, unselfish, and patriotic. If you are brave, unselfish, and patriotic, you will never be a drunkard. So Mama's piece *is* a temperance piece, even though there are no drunkards in it." This was pure logic; but at twelve, I, a logician myself, already knew that not many people paid any attention to logic.

One thing was in Birdeen's favor. She was next to

the last, and everyone agreed that if you were good, the later you spoke, the better. By that time, the judges' memories had begun to slip about how good the first speakers had been. Marie Ashton, I was happy to see, was third on the program.

I had planned to seat myself between Neddie and Ramona on purpose. I didn't want to sit next to Reno. I did take a look at him when he came in. There was nothing to be learned from his appearance. He had on his best suit and tie. He smelled of shaving soap. But from anything his face showed, he might have been sitting in church—ready once more to sing "Sweet Marie." I did not believe that my father was gifted with finer feelings.

The four of us were sitting in the section labeled "Contestants' Families." Zen had decided how we would sit: he and I in the middle, Neddie next to him and Ramona next to me.

Reno, when he came in, sat next to Neddie. There was no use asking so calm a man how Birdeen was. He wouldn't have noticed. I felt sick at my stomach with excitement.

The church organist came in from the Sunday-school room, which opened onto the stage, gave the organ stool a few quick spins upward, then a couple of slow turns downward. She seated herself, adjusted her glasses, her music, her cuffs and, last of all, took off her rings. Then she looked at the door of the Sunday-school room, and saw something hidden from the audience, for she lifted her hands and arched her wrists. She waited, and when everyone least expected it, hit a triumphant chord. The back of my neck got cold. The elocution ladies came in, all in white, each wearing a pink rosebud, all locked together in the cause of temperance by a rope of smilax and maidenhair fern that they carried.

There was no letdown. The lady contestants filed onto the stage, solemnly, excitingly, murmurously. Their skirts rustled; they smelled sweet, as far as the fifth row, anyway. In addition to their pink rosebuds, they wore all the lockets, brooches, rings, and watches they possessed. Birdeen had the tightest belt, the smallest waist, the whitest face, the brightest eyes, the curliest hair.

Some of the ladies looked straight ahead, like soldiers on guard duty; some smiled at the audience like actresses; some gazed at the floor as if engaged in prayer. The ten could have reached their chairs in two seconds if they had taken a direct route, or walked at their ordinary gait. They didn't do either. First, they all walked behind the chairs, which gave them twice as far to go; then, between each step, they stopped dead still for a moment, which took them twice as long. I supposed it was done to give the judges a chance to grade them on dress, stage presence, demeanor, and grace. It gave me sweaty hands. Even when the contestants reached their chairs, they didn't sit. They stood. The audience stood. The Reverend Bewley Cope prayed that the occasion might be a source of blessing to all and to drunkards especially. Everyone then sat; but still the contest didn't begin. Jess Carson sang "On the Road to Mandalay" and Mary Alice Able followed with "Just A-Wearyin' for You."

My head began to ache. I felt the occasion was too serious for singing and, until my mother was safely through her piece with the silver medal pinned on her shirtwaist, I didn't have the heart for music. Besides, it reminded me of my dream. Marie Ashton was up there on the stage just as I had dreamed, and Reno was down in the audience. What if my dream had foretold the future, as even the Bible said dreams did? And *now* was the time Reno would rise to his feet, make his lovesick bow to Marie, and begin *his* solo. I glanced at my father sidewise, but I couldn't tell whether he was looking at Marie Ashton or Birdeen.

During the singing, I nervously reviewed my mother's chances of winning. Besides Marie Ashton, there were three contestants who were dangerous: Lady Anne Bluett, Ella McBride, and Clara Carmody.

Lady Anne Bluett wouldn't have had much of a chance in anything but a temperance contest. In the first place, she didn't speak up so you could hear her. But in her case, this was thought to be a good sign. It proved that what *she* said wasn't make-believe, that every word came all the way from her heart; and no wonder she could do no more than whisper. *She* was a bona-fide drunkard's wife, and half the time had a black eye to prove it. Thank goodness her eyes were all right to-night. She made the judges' work hard. If they gave the medal to someone else, it was like saying that a lie was better than the truth.

Ella McBride was a music teacher, and her recitation was always half music. She went down to the organ to say her piece, reciting the words over her shoulder while she kept her eyes on keys, stops, and sheet music. Like Lady Anne Bluett, she was hard to hear, but it was remarkable that anyone should be able to do so many things at once: feet pumping the bellows in and out; fingers pulling stops, pushing keys, and turning pages; voice reciting her story. She was always a grand sight, as exciting to watch as a sack race. She worried me.

So did Clara Carmody. Mrs. Carmody was a dressmaker, and what she enjoyed most about the elocution contests was the chance it gave her to make and wear a costume. She made wonderful clothes. It was as good as a trip abroad to see her. I could remember her as a Highland lassie, an Irish bog trotter, a veiled woman of Algiers. No one could understand one word she said the night she was veiled. And at all times, it was difficult. It wasn't that she whispered like Lady Anne, or got drowned out by the organ like Ella McBride. Mrs. Carmody was loud. You could hear her clear down the road. What you couldn't do was understand her. She spoke in a dialect to match her costume; she was so thorough, no one but another bog-trotter or Algerian *could* understand her. The judges were always of two minds about this. Maybe the point of a dialect was that it couldn't be understood. Perhaps they were being unfair to Mrs. Carmody. Giving her low grades for what was really her long suit. Mrs. Carmody had never won a contest yet, and I knew the judges felt guilty about it. No one worked as hard as she did. She deserved to win on her costumes alone, to say nothing of those jawbreakers she was letter-perfect in saying. Was understanding so important? What if they were judging a contest in a foreign land? They wouldn't be able to understand a word. Mrs. Carmody brought a foreign land to them. This could be the night the judges, no matter how good everyone else was, decided to make it up to Mrs. Carmody for overlooking her so many times in the past.

I, when the first contestant was announced, cupped my brow in my palm, as if in prayer. I wasn't praying. I was sending out thought waves to the judges. Besides possibly helping Mama, my thought waves kept me from hearing the recitations and the applause of the audience. Some things, of course, I couldn't help from knowing. I knew that Lily White's memory failed her half through her piece, and that Lily White had to sit down.

Neither prayer nor closed eyes prevented me from knowing when Marie Ashton began her piece. I stopped looking like I was praying when Mrs. Ashton came to

" 'That was before I got to tipplin'
And gin got in my nose.' "

I stopped not because of the words, with which I was familiar, but because of the sounds Zen was making: a man tickled to death, but for politeness' sake trying to hold back the laughter. The snorts and chuckles kept breaking through, though unblameworthy because everybody could tell that Zen was almost strangling to death in his effort to be polite. If Zen had been a local rancher, the audience might have thought he was a yokel who couldn't recognize good elocution and a telling phrase when he heard it. As it was, since a big car dealer from Santa Ana had done the laughing, perhaps there was something ridiculous in the piece they had missed, so they laughed a little themselves.

Marie Ashton had spunk. She stumbled a little at the laughter, then went right on.

" 'Come give me my glass now, Colonel,
    And I'll be on my way.
    And I'll tromp 'til I catch that scoundrel
    If it takes 'til Judgment Day.' "

The audience, ashamed of itself for laughing, and admiring Mrs. Ashton's courage, clapped loudly.

Don't judge yet, I signaled the judges with my thought waves. The best is yet to come. Wait for "Kentucky Belle." I put my hand over my face in order to concentrate better in advising the judges.

My father, reaching across Neddie and Zen, gave me a hard pinch. "Ginerva, that don't look good, hiding your face when the speakers recite," he whispered.

"I am thinking victory," I whispered back.

"I don't care what you're thinking. Take your hand down."

I took it down. I looked at Birdeen, and she looked back. I said with my eyes, "Your dreams will come true." It was knowing so much about these dreams that made me motherly at twelve.

Birdeen had walked around from the very beginning of her life dreaming that she was a bird in flight, a bride in a girl, a poet in a book; and, when she went to church and sang "I am a pilgrim in a foreign land," she was a pilgrim in a foreign land. Now she hoped for the very best—Haviland china, inlaid Wilton, a Kurtzman piano, an inside toilet, a taffeta-silk petticoat. And her teeth fixed. Birdeen, who quickly lost her temper, talked crazy on purpose, couldn't bear pain, worked too hard, and wanted to be a good woman. She was also a prize-winning elocutionist with a fashionable hairdo, as anyone could see.

At last Birdeen rose to her feet, advanced to the edge of the platform, and there was nothing to fear. The other women had been up there on that platform, remembering with ease or difficulty, reciting clearly or indistinctly, rating from 0 to 20 for appearance. Birdeen Chalmers *was* her recitation, the way a bird is its song, or a rabbit is its hop.

"I want to tell you," she said, in her voice that promised magic and sorrow, but did not exclude hope, "the story of Kentucky Belle."

Then Birdeen Chalmers vanished. No, she was there, but she was there as the sun is on a fine day. It's the light and the warmth you notice, not the sun.

I followed, as I had promised my mother I would, the recitation word by word. But I was hearing a new story, the story the woman, not Birdeen, the woman in the poem, was telling.

"Morgan," this woman who was young and frightened and a Southerner told them, "Morgan the raider and Morgan's terrible men . . . and on came the soldiers, the Michigan cavalry, and fast they rode and black they looked, galloping rapidly . . . and the boy, worn out with his ride with Morgan up from Tennessee . . . well, I kept the boy 'til evening, kept him against his will . . . when it was cool and dusky, you'll wonder to hear me tell, I stole down to the gully and brought up Kentucky Belle."

There wasn't going to be a bit of temperance in the story to please the W.C.T.U., nor a bit of peace to please the Christians, and not very much "hurrah for our side" to please the patriots. There would be no dialect to make folks wonder how the human tongue could wrap itself around such jawbreakers. There was no death and failure to make them think they were listening to something deep like Shakespeare. Nothing but the story of a woman, who was doing her best, with good results for all. This, the good results, was, of course, not to be given to the audience until the last verse; thus enhancing the pleasure of wondering and worrying. And each person felt, listening, that life had asked too little of him; that given the chance, he, too, could go down that country road hazarding his life and his horse. Birdeen's poem made everyone there a hero. Not a housewife or rancher in the crowd— not a soul there—but became big-hearted, chance-takers, listening to Birdeen.

I knew by the time she was halfway through that my mother had won. Even the faces of the other contestants showed it. Lily White, who had been brave about her own mix-up, was crying for "Kentucky Belle." Marie Ashton looked as if she'd just got news her house was on fire.

Birdeen had only three more stanzas to say.

"Kentuck," she said in her voice of love and memory, "pretty Kentuck, I gave to that worn-out lad."

Then Birdeen took a step backward, reached for her chair, finally got hold of it, and stood swaying. Some people thought it was a part of the recitation. I knew better. I stood up as my mother's hand came loose from the chair and she slid, first to her knees, then face downward on the floor.

Papa and I reached the platform at the same time. I knew *that,* but knew nothing else of what went on behind me. I stepped into my mother's place, and in her voice, which I had by nature, and with her intonation, which I had picked up in the hours I had listened to her practice, I said, "Kentuck, pretty Kentuck, I gave to that worn-out lad, and I guided the boy to the southward as well as I knew how." There were tears on my face for the cause and the horse that were lost.

Birdeen's fainting didn't worry me. She was an easy fainter, keeled over and came to in fifteen minutes feeling refreshed. Birdeen fainted the way other people took a nap. She wouldn't take a rest of her own free will. Nature gave her a rest by letting her lie down unconscious for a few minutes. Nature didn't care whether Birdeen was in the middle of an elocution contest or not. Reno had Birdeen in his arms and was out the door before I had finished parting with Kentucky Belle.

The judges came to a decision in no time at all. They didn't mention Birdeen, just said, "By unanimous decision, first place is awarded to Ginerva Chalmers for 'Kentucky Belle.'" Then Mr. Elmer Tracy pinned the silver medal on my dress, clear through to the skin on the first try.

Though all of my family except Zen had gone home, I stayed on for the refreshments. It didn't seem polite to win a medal and run. The refreshments were homemade chocolate ice cream, my favorite, and jelly-roll cake.

Marie Ashton was beaten, which was a good thing, whoever did it. And Keno had seen that Marie couldn't hold a candle to Birdeen. But what if Birdeen would have won the medal anyway? What if I hadn't jumped up there and finished "Kentucky Belle" for her? Birdeen, who could come to in fifteen minuts, might have been able in an emergency like this to come to in a flash. What if she had sprung to her feet and gone on with her recitation, a soldier wounded on the field of battle but refusing to give up? Wouldn't Birdeen have won the medal for elocution? And one for bravery, besides?

I unpinned the medal from my dress and turned it round and round in my hand. What had possessed me to jump up there and begin reciting almost before my mother had hit the floor? The contest had come out the right way—with Marie Ashton licked—but would Birdeen want to owe the medal to a twelve-year-old, even if she was her own daughter? And if you took the judges' word for it, that was the case. They didn't even mention Birdeen's name.

Marie Ashton, with Zen by her side, came up to congratulate me.

"Well, pin it on, winner," she said, taking the medal from my hand and pinning it on just as skin deep as Elmer Tracy had done. "This was a night for the Chalmers family. You reciting and Zen here laughing at drinking like it was something comical."

"Now, Marie, you know I'd never do that. Tippling is serious and I treat it that way."

"You telling me, Zen." If Mrs. Ashton had had an parasol, she would, I was sure, have given Zen a poke with it. As it was, she had nothing but her finger. It was half a punch, half a tickle. "Since you're so sober, how about taking me home? Al's at a Masonic meeting. Liquor's not Al's problem."

"You telling me, Marie," Zen said. "It'd be my pleasure, but I've promised to see my niece home."

I wondered who he'd promised, but didn't think this was the time to ask. Marie Ashton had had her second comedown of the evening, but there was no point rubbing it in.

Outside, the air, which had cooled at sunset, had warmed up again. A Santa Ana was brewing. Already, from the row of eucalyptus that had been planted as a windbreak for the grove on the other side of the church came a soft surflike rumble. The orange trees were beginning to rustle.

Zen opened the door of his car for me, something that he had never done before. Being a winner impressed him.

"How about a little spin, Aunt Jetty? Cool you off and settle you down?"

"Not 'til we tell Mama we've won."

At home, Birdeen was stretched out on the living-room davenport, a pillow at her head and a glass of lemonade on the taboret by her side. Reno, coat and tie off, was at the east window trying to pick up a whiff of the Santa Ana, which wasn't cool but had, because it was moving, the feel of coolness.

"Have some lemonade, Zen?" Reno invited.

"It's been a dry evening," Zen said. "Lemonade would be better than nothing."

"How are you, Mama?" I asked.

"Why, you know how these spells hit me. They're gone in a minute and I feel better afterward."

"Mama," I went on in a rush, "here is the medal for the best recitation. The judges sent it home by me."

I held the medal toward her, but Birdeen made no move to take it.

"It's your medal, Mama."

"That's not what the judges said."

"How do you know, Mama?"

Reno, who had come back from the kitchen with Zen and lemonade for both of them, answered the question. "In the best way possible. By seeing and hearing."

"How could you? You went home."

"We rested up long enough in the Sunday-school room to hear what went on."

"Mama, could you have gone on? You couldn't, could you?" I pleaded.

"What chance did she have with you up there spouting?" Reno demanded.

"I did it for you, Mama. I did it to beat Marie Ashton."

"Marie Ashton?" Birdeen asked.

"You know that, don't you, Papa?"

If he did, he didn't admit it. "Your mother had Marie Ashton licked from the word go and without any help from you."

"How did I know she would come to so soon?"

"You didn't waste any time waiting to see. You must

have Roosevelt blood in your veins, Ginerva. They say Teddy's got to be the bride at the wedding and the corpse at the funeral. At an elocution contest, he'd be the elocutionist, too. Like you."

It wasn't true. All I tried to do at all times was to be Mama's helper.

"Oh, Mama," I lamented, "why did you have to pick tomatoes today?"

"Pick tomatoes?" Birdeen asked, bridling. "Are you in cahoots with your father, blaming me for that?"

In cahoots with my father? I felt bewildered. Reno and I weren't even on good terms.

I held out the medal once again. "It's yours, Mama."

Birdeen shook her head. "You won it. Wear it."

I went to the open window beside which Zen stood. "If you don't want it, I don't, either," I said. I threw the medal as far as I could into the back yard.

Birdeen jumped to her feet, and for a minute I thought I was due for one of her quick flashing slaps. But she was interested in the medal itself. She was peering out the window as if she might catch sight of the gleam of the silver medal she had never won.

"Throwing away valuables! There's a Chalmers for you if I ever saw one."

I had never before fallen so far out of favor with my mother. Being a Chalmers was as much as to say that I wasn't even of Mama's own blood.

Our voices, not quiet, had roused Ramona from sleep.

At the top of the stairs she called, "Ginny, I've got the earache."

I would have run to a pinprick call. I scooped up

Ramona at the head of the stairs, carried her to her own bed and cuddled her. "Oh, Ramona, poor little Ramona, poor, poor Ramona," I said.

Ramona finally wiggled out of my arms. "Why are you crying, Ginny?"

"Because I'm so sorry for us, Ramona."

"My ear don't hurt that bad."

I went back to cuddling and crying and rocking. "Papa and Mama don't love us, Ramona."

"They love me," Ramona said. "You're making my ear wet."

When I didn't answer, Ramona said, "I need a glass of water."

For that, I had to go downstairs again. On the landing, I could hear Reno and Birdeen, who had come up to bed, laughing. Laughing! Laughing, while my heart was breaking!

"Oh, forget Ginerva," my father was saying. "She's no Chalmers, and you know it. Pure McManus. She'll be down there hunting for that medal before we're out of bed in the morning."

"Finding it, too, I'll bet," Birdeen said.

"What'd I tell you?" Reno asked. "Pure McManus."

I didn't wait to hear any more. I will not, I told myself as I went down the stairs. I will never take one step to see where that medal is as long as I live. I could still hear them laughing and talking. Hearing them, I made myself another promise. And I will never try to help anyone again as long as I live, either. I will live for myself.

In the kitchen, there stood Zen. "When are we going to take that spin?" he asked.

"I didn't know you'd wait."

"I'll always wait. What's the glass for?"

"Water. Ramona has the earache."

"That's a queer cure for the earache. I'll be here when you come back down."

Zen said, "Let's head for the beach."

The ocean scared me. It was a big snake, a big slippery snake curled round the world. I loved water—water that could be managed, water running from a weir box into the standpipes, then down the irrigation ditches between the orange trees. I loved the Santa Ana River, a stream that had to struggle to escape being swallowed by the earth long before it reached the sea.

The ocean wasn't like the manageable water ranchers put into a reservoir, or a creek that dried up in years when there wasn't much rain. It wasn't dependent on man or rain. It was alive. It moved about, regular as a heartbeat; but it didn't always promise life, as a heartbeat did.

At high tide, the sea could smash buildings; with its undertow, it could drag swimmers out beyond any returning. From a high cliff, it was a pleasure to watch; but it was no more to be fooled with than a rattlesnake.

"There'll be some dampness down there to offset the sand this wind is making us eat."

I said nothing.

"You okay?" Zen asked.

Fear of the sea was one of my secrets. And who would believe that a girl who would rush up onto a public platform and demand the attention that rightly belonged to her mother could be afraid of something as natural as water?

"Did I do wrong, Uncle Zen?"

"There must've been times, I reckon."

"I mean tonight."

"Doing what?"

"Speaking Mama's piece."

"What was wrong with that?"

"Like I was hunting the limelight."

"The limelight was where it had to be said."

"I could've sat still and kept my mouth shut."

"I misdoubt that was possible. Likely not best, either."

"What makes you think that?"

"Experience."

"Did you ever recite someone else's piece?"

"One not my own, anyway. And I didn't win any medal, either."

7

Try not to tell her that long-winded story, Zen told himself. You don't understand your own acts yourself; how
expect her to?

The wind, funneling through a break in the Coyote
hills, hit the Hup a staggering blow.

"Will we blow over?" Ginerva asked.

"Not a chance," Zen replied. "How would you like
to learn to drive?"

"Am I old enough?"

"Plenty old. With a good teacher like me."

"Not tonight."

"What do you want to do tonight?"

"Remember."

"Well, that suits me, too."

Ginerva leaned closer to Zen. Asleep probably, he thought,
after the evening she'd been through. Poor kid. She'd
done her best—just as she did when little more than a
baby to help me with Love Lewis.

What a different life he would have had if Love had
lived. Or Mary, for that matter. Love Lewis, Mary
Graves: Love and Graves. If he had another life, he'd
pay more attention to names. He'd been called a "lady
killer"; yes, he should have paid more attention to names.
Love had died before they were married; Mary, eleven
months afterward. A sane man, and there were times
when Zen wasn't sure he qualified as such, would have

told himself that he was unlucky. But Zen could not.

He felt guilty. Love died of the same illness that had sent him to California. There was no more reason to think he'd given it to her than she had given it to him; but reasoning wasn't his long suit after Love's death.

Not after Mary's death, either. What killed Mary *was* the result of what he'd given her: a baby, stillborn, and Mary herself dead after two and a half days of labor.

He felt guilty after those two deaths and in great need of forgiveness—love and forgiveness beyond anything there was to be had from the Lewises, the Graveses, or the McManuses, though they gave him what they had. What he needed was something no human had. So he started going to church, hunting a love and forgiveness there he had never felt the need of before.

He had to admit that there was something there, something he had never found anywhere else. God?

Well, it certainly wasn't the congregation. They were —some of them, anyway—inclined to believe that God had sacrificed Love and Mary for the same reason He had asked Abraham to sacrifice Isaac: to advance the Kingdom. Those two girls had died; their deaths had caused a man who had never set his foot in church to do so. It was God's work, wasn't it? Not any God Zen knew anything about.

Ginerva slumped more heavily against him. Zen supported her with his arm. They were about five or six miles from the sea. He had a longing for which he couldn't account to have a look at that great heaving body of water. It called to him the way God had in his churchgoing days.

"I was hunting God when I started going to church, but Lavelle thought I was hunting her."

It was only a thought, but he spoke the words, without intending to, aloud. They didn't rouse Ginerva. Would she have understood the ludicrous account of the time when he had spoken another's words with far worse results than anything she had accomplished with her medal-winning performance? He thought so—she, with her McManus mind and Love Lewis face.

When Zen, in sorrow and loneliness, started going to church, Lavelle Saunders, the local schoolmarm, was keeping company with Lafe Tetlow. Lafe's full name was Lafayette, and he owned a half-interest in the Brush Creek General Store. That was about the last thing Lafe ever owned a half-interest in.

Lafe was born to be a prosperous merchant, and even then had the right look for the role. Zen was surprised that he could remember so well the faces of those who had sat with him in the Brush Creek Church. He could still see Lafe's little sparkling brown eyes, exaggerated cowlick, and mouth like the opening of a coin purse: a small coin purse with a snapcatch. Lafe came to church early in order to start the fire. He was good at it: a combination of birch and hickory—birch to go forward, hickory to hold back. The result was a fire like a foundry's and a fine warm room when the congregation arrived.

Lavelle, as organist, came early, too, in order to have the songbooks, hers and the congregation's, in order. Zen was there early because, as a young widower, an empty bed on Sunday morning was the loneliest place in the world. He craved a cure for his broken heart, and he thought God could give it to him.

Lavelle thought she could.

After they were married, Lavelle told Zen about her first conversation with Lafe about him.

"Lafe said you were a man like a mule. I told Lafe you didn't look it."

"What did I look like to you?"

"A pirate or a highwayman. Or a Johnny Reb."

" 'Any of those wrongdoers ladies fancy,' Lafe said. Then Lafe added, 'Looks more like a splinter to me.' "

"I agreed. 'Splinter of a newly felled pine.' Lafe got the picture. Taffy-colored, full of resin, sweet-smelling, inflammable, ready to go off like a Roman candle."

Zen did not find God, but being, as Lafe had said, a man like a mule, he kept on trying. Meanwhile, Lavelle found Zen.

She asked him to come to her home after the Protracted Meeting. The visiting preacher was to be honored by an ice-cream supper at the Saunders home.

"Your father isn't going to like that."

"I'm preparing him for it."

Old Levi Saunders was a shouting atheist, the way there are shouting drunks and shouting Methodists. Levi didn't believe there was a God, and he didn't believe in sitting back and doing nothing about it. He was a preacher operating in reverse gear. He was a would-be martyr crying out for burning, but nobody in Brush Creek was so serious about religion that he'd get together enough faggots for the burning. Derision, scorn, contempt; the merest chaff to a real martyr, flies to flinch off. What Levi wanted was an eagle with its beak in his liver.

It was maddening to Levi that not even God paid him any heed. No bolts of lightning to strike him down, no plagues to wipe out his flocks. He and his family prospered in a way to prove positively that God didn't exist. No God worth His salt would put up with Levi's insubordination. Old Levi never would have, certainly. Churchgoing Lavelle was perhaps God's way of saying to Levi, "Your time is short. I've got eternity to work in."

Zen wasn't drawn to Lavelle as a substitute for Love or Mary. But he was lonesome and God-hungry and Lavelle had arrived at the destination he was headed for.

"I don't like to upset your father."

"I told you I'd prepared him. The Reverend Gower will be there. He's speaking on 'Tomorrow—What Will It Mean to Me?' I'd hate to miss it."

"If it's no better than yesterday, I'll take a miss."

They all took a miss. The Reverend Gower, exhorting in Carolltown, came down with quinsy, and the Protracted Meeting was postponed. Not Zen's invitation, though. "I've baked a White Mountain cake especially for you."

"Your pa?"

"He'll be in bed."

He appeared to be so. The fire in the grate had been banked. The parlor lamp had been turned so low its light scarcely yellowed the room.

"You sit down," Zen told Lavelle, "and I'll help you off with your overshoes." Her shoes, too, were damp, and Zen stayed on his knees helping her off with them.

Neither saw the old man, silhouetted in the doorway, until he spoke. In his long white undershirt, he looked like Moses, except that instead of graven tablets he carried his two shoes in his hand.

"Off your knees," he thundered. "That's not a posture I'll permit in my house. Pray in church if you want to. Pray in your own house. That's your castle. But this is my castle, and there's not going to be any mumbo-jumbo of that kind in my parlor while I'm able to defend myself."

Zen, unable to resist the attraction of mischief, began, when forbidden, to pray.

"Good Lord," he prayed in the resonant baritone thin men often have, "note here Thy poor servant. Consider his extremity. Protect him from the wrath of his oppressor. Save him from the pestilence that walks by night."

Praying was bad enough, but being prayed against, called a night-walking pestilence in his own parlor, was a pass to which Levi had never expected to come.

"Don't say you haven't been warned," he rumbled. "Get up on your two feet, and I'll let bygones be bygones."

Zen, who had not yet found God, couldn't let Him be a bygone. He prayed on. His voice continued unbroken in piety and swelling in volume.

Levi was the one used to making the noise in that house. "I'm against force," he bellowed. "It ain't rational. But what you're doing ain't rational, either."

He flung a shoe, with more force than aim, missed Zen, his target, and hit the fire. Old Levi kept his shoes well larded with mutton fat. The flames licked round his boot as if it had been pitch pine.

"Yank it out," he yelled, since Zen and Lavelle blocked his way.

Zen prayed on.

The old man was hissing like a gander.

"Off your haunches, Reverend," he bellowed. "Get off your holy haunches or be prepared to take the consequences."

Lavelle, also screaming, was able to be heard above the tumult of praying and antipraying.

"His haunches aren't holy, Pa."

Zen prayed on.

Levi's second boot was better aimed than the first. It hit Zen amidships with a rib-cracking kerplunk.

"Lord," Zen said, "they know not what they do."

Lavelle leaped toward her father. Next, he would be wrapping a stove poker around Zen's head.

"Get the Reverend out of here," Levi yelled.

"It's not the Reverend. Turn up the lamp and see."

"You said you were bringing the Reverend Gower home."

"I couldn't. He's down with the quinsy."

"Who's this?"

"Turn up the lamp."

"Zen McManus! What're you doing here?"

"Seeing your daughter home."

"Sparking! That's more like it. Sounded like prayer to me. I'd of sworn you were praying."

"I was seeing your daughter home from church."

"Fine thing. She's still a teacher at twenty-four. Bad business for a woman. Draws all the blood to the head."

"He was proposing," said Lavelle.

"Is that a fact?" asked Levi.

It wasn't, but Zen, who had suffered a lot himself, didn't have the heart to call the girl a liar before her own father.

"What was your answer, daughter?"

"Yes," said Lavelle. She put her arms around Zen. "I've been waiting for a long time for the right man, and I found him where I knew I would. In church."

Zen had been hunting God in church, not another wife. But he was hungrier than he'd had any idea for a girl's arms and, under the circumstances, he didn't have the heart to ask her to take them down.

"I'd never give up the right to pray, Mr. Saunders, when I pleased."

"When's okay. It's where, I'm talking about."

"I'd try not to tread on your toes in your own house." He wanted to add, "Except when you've thrown your shoes at me," but managed to keep his mouth shut.

"Oh, this is the happiest day of my life," Lavelle said.

It may have been. It certainly wasn't very happy after that.

Zen had been able to remember that evening of praying and lying and proposing as funny. It hadn't been funny. It was pitiful. A man so stricken with the loss of the two girls he had loved that he believed he could find a substitute in God. Believed that until he felt a girl's arms about him. The only straight shooter that evening had been old Levi himself, and even he got confused when he saw the chance of saving his daughter from spinster-hood.

When he reached the Huntington Beach pier, Zen pulled up. He could see, smell, and hear the ocean, and that was all he had come for. The stopping of the car awakened Ginerva.

"Where are we?" she asked.

"The beach."

"I was dreaming."

"Me, too, though I wasn't asleep."

"Was it a nice dream?"

"No. Sad."

"About Love Lewis?"

"No. Lavelle."

"The one who divorced you?"

"I divorced her."

"Why?"

"She hoodwinked me. Forget it. It's over and done with. Look at the ocean. Look at the moon. You'd never think, would you, that that sliver of light up there could make the ocean rise and fall."

"I don't like to look at the ocean. It scares me."

"You never go swimming. How can the ocean harm you?"

"A tidal wave could. It comes after people and kills them."

"California doesn't have tidal waves."

"It's going to. I heard the men talking. They're pumping so much oil out from under the land that the land will cave in and the ocean will run in to take its place. I listen every night for a tidal wave. I never go to bed without remembering where things that float are."

"Like what?"

108

"Tubs. Benches. Lumber left over from the house."

"You going to float off alone?"

"Of course not. I'll get Neddie and Ramona in a tub."

"What about your folks?"

"Mama will look after Papa."

"Your mother can't swim a stroke."

"She'll find something for them to float on."

"You're your mother's girl, aren't you?"

"I think she can do anything she puts her mind to."

"Your father does, too, so you got some Chalmers blood in you, Aunt Jetty."

The moon that pulled the waves was already down when they got home, but out in the back yard with a flashlight was Reno, scratching around to find the thrown-away medal. He found it just as they joined him.

"Ginerva, you take this in to your mother. She worked for weeks to prepare herself, outshone everyone, then you threw it all away." Reno's voice was loud and harsh.

Ginerva took the medal and ran inside.

"What're you doing out this time of night with my daughter, Zen?"

"She was wrought up after the contest. We went for a spin to cool off."

"Cool off, with this wind blowing?"

"We went to the beach."

"Zen, you're my wife's brother. That doesn't blind me to your reputation. Now, no more spins with my daughter."

There was one blow struck. Reno set Zen down onto the ground where he had been searching for the medal.

No bones broken, but Zen was too dizzy to care. Then Reno went into the house.

When Zen got up, he said to himself, That was some spin. He could brush the dirt off, but the blood from his swollen nose would take water.

He was about six hours late for his date with Sarah Loomis, but Sarah wasn't the kind of woman who expected life to run on schedule like a train.

"You been in an accident, Zen?" she asked.

"You might say so."

"Got the worst of it, too."

"You might say so."

"Well, come on in. Get washed up and something to eat."

He needed washing up. He needed food. He had spent at least two nights out of each seven at Sarah's during the last year. Sarah hadn't been in any accident, but her looks had somehow changed. She was forty. The word for her was blowsy. She wasn't fat, but her flesh wasn't very firmly attached to her bones. She was, though he hadn't noticed it before, carrot-colored. She used cotton flannel sheets on her bed; and changed them when she got around to it. If the ocean meant anything to her, or any fish in it or ship on it, she'd never mentioned the fact.

"No," Zen said. "I just stopped by to tell you I wouldn't be able to make it tonight. A hot tub and Sloane's liniment is about all I need tonight."

"That's what you stopped to tell me?"

"That's the message, I guess."

8

The medal felt hot in my hand. It wasn't any bigger than a two-bit piece and even lighter. As I mounted the stairs to my parents' room, I turned the medal over and over in my hand. I heard through the window at the head of the stairs the voices of Reno and Zen.

The Women's Christian Temperance Union certainly worked for good. Persuading men not to be drunkards was surely a good thing. Work of that kind *should* fill the hearts of its members with happiness. But Birdeen had fainted speaking her piece. Zen had snickered at sweet Marie's recitation. My own father had berated me for finishing in Birdeen's place and had thought that selfishness caused me to take the medal. Then I had thrown the medal away.

And now, to cap the climax, Reno and Zen, their voices as loud as any drunkards', were bellowing at each other. The roosters had stopped crowing to listen.

My mother was wide awake, propped high against the headboard of her bed. She couldn't help but hear the arguing, but she didn't seem troubled by it. She was wearing her special-occasions nightgown, the one for Christmas morning or visiting in-laws.

"Petty," Birdeen said, "you're not still worrying about that medal, are you?"

"Not now. I brought it to you."

"I knew you would. I knew you would. That was just McManus high spirits, throwing it out the window."

Finding it was Chalmers good sense, and I thought she would say so. She didn't.

She turned the medal over and over in her hand. "Together we did it, didn't we?"

"I jumped up too fast."

"It was then or never."

"Papa thought it was too fast—that I should have waited until you came to."

"You did the right thing. The medal proves it. How did anyone know I was going to come to? And who wants to give a medal to someone with a bottle of smelling salts clapped to her nose?"

"Did Papa want sweet Marie to win it?"

"Petty, don't be crazy. He wanted me to win it. But he's a Chalmers. He's the best and handsomest father a girl could have. You upset him by running up onto the stage. You were a show-off by Chalmers's standards."

"What would a Chalmers have done?"

"Nothing. Not entered the contest. Not picked tomatoes. Not fainted."

"Not won a medal."

"What's a medal? Your papa's right. We're show-offs and not happy unless we come in first. It's fun to be first, but it won't save the world."

"It *was* fun, wasn't it, Mama?"

"It was fun and we did it, but that don't make your papa wrong. I wouldn't trade him for a bushel of medals. You get to bed now. If we're going to stay up all night, we're acting like drunkards ourselves. What's that noise below in the yard?"

"Papa and Uncle Zen."

"What's Zen doing here?"

"After he told you good night, he didn't go home."

"He'll go home now or I'll miss my guess. Reno's no hand for all-night palaver. You get to bed now."

9

Reno was blood-spattered when he came up to bed. Since he had nosebleeds about as often as she fainted, Birdeen never suspected fisticuffs.

"Fainting and nosebleeds," Birdeen said. "We're a sorry lot."

"I wouldn't deny that, but this is no nosebleed."

"You're bleeding. What caused that?"

"Your brother Zen. But don't blame him. I bet his ear's still ringing."

"There's nothing wrong with Zen's ears."

"There is now. Bang on the head, then bang on the ground."

"Who did that?"

"Me. The blood you see is Zen's. But he sure asked for it. Traipsing around half the night with Ginerva."

"Traipsing around?"

"Took her to the beach, for one thing."

"For one thing?"

"You know your brother's reputation as well as I do."

"How did you find out about it?"

"They came in just as I was hunting your medal."

"Ginerva had already found it."

"Is that what she told you?"

"She didn't say a word. Just handed me the medal."

"And you thought that while I was fighting your brother, Ginerva was out hunting your precious medal."

Birdeen leaped from her bed and gave the medal a second mighty fling into the back yard.

"I never called it precious once in my life."

Reno sat down in Birdeen's sewing rocker, which she kept near the window where the light was good. All that medal-throwing made him laugh.

"Well, I sure hope you hit near the same spot where I found it before."

"Oh, Reno, don't you wish you'd married a good-hearted Christian girl?"

"I did, I did," Reno said, "and sometimes I wish I hadn't. No Christian Temperance meetings. No tomato picking to pay the bills. Just an easygoing Chalmers slut. That's my style."

Birdeen threw herself onto Reno's lap.

"Don't say that, Reno. I never called a relative of yours a slut. And you wouldn't be happy with one."

"I wouldn't be happy with anyone but you and that's a cinch."

Reno stroked the pink-sprigged nightgown. "What's this special nightgown for? This some special kind of night?"

"Yes, it's special."

"I didn't notice any date on the calendar."

"It's a date in my heart."

"Don't tell me I've forgotten another anniversary."

"Yes, you have. The hundredth time. We've had words and are sorry for it. That's what we're celebrating."

"You're right," said Reno. He picked up Birdeen and carried her to their bed.

10

Standing at the kitchen sink of his house, Zen washed his brother-in-law's "gift" from his face. He took off his blood-spattered shirt and planned to go to bed in his B.V.D.'s. But it was an odd hour to go to bed: roosters almost finished with crowing, twilight becoming daylight.

'Bout as well make a night of it, he told himself. He pulled his pants back on and put a couple of tablespoonfuls of Arbuckle's coffee in the coffeepot. The coffee brought him into a daylight state, tired but no longer sleepy. Liquor he could do without, but he'd hate to try to live without coffee.

He was into his second cup when Sarah Loomis came in without knocking. Sarah was the postmistress at Valencia, the town of two thousand where the ranchers and their wives did their shopping. Easterners settling in California began, as soon as they learned the strange names of California fruits, to name their towns for them: Orange and Olive and Loquat. Navels were larger and handsomer oranges than Valencias. But who wants to be a resident of Navel?

Sarah had never been in Zen's house before, and Zen didn't want her here now.

"Who's taking care of the mail today?" he asked.

"There's a substitute in case of emergency."

"What's the emergency today?"

"You, I reckon."

"Join the emergency in a cup of coffee."

She poured herself a cup and sat at the table with him.

"I oughtn't to be here."

Zen didn't disagree with her and he didn't need to. She had a pretty good idea why at forty she wasn't married. She was no prize beauty, but Valencia was filled with flat-chested straggle-haired women who had had no trouble catching husbands. What was the trouble with her?

The trouble, she knew well enough, was in the word "catch." No one had had to catch her. And men didn't value what they didn't have to pursue. The whole worlds of hunting and of sport, men's greatest pleasures, were based on pursuit. Getting something that didn't want to be caught, that eluded them: a running deer, a cannonball pitch, a resisting woman. Sarah was short on resistance.

Look at her now. No woman had ever been given a more bald-faced brush-off than Zen had given her. A date of long standing walked out on without apology. Where was her pride? If she wasn't able to assume the pretense of resistance men loved, didn't she at least have some self-respect? Evidently not.

Zen poured his third cup of coffee and waited, she supposed, to hear whatever it was she had come over to say. It wouldn't be news to him. It had already been said. Her job given up for the day, a tromp across town to be near him, emphasized it.

Zen was a stringy man, big eyes, long lashes, a mouth that liked words and women. She was bolder with acts than with words. Everything she had done had said, "I love you, Zen McManus."

The words she spoke were only, "What has happened?"

"I had a little misunderstanding with my brother-in-law."

"I mean, between us."

"Nothing."

"That's what I mean. All at once?"

"I got a pretty good jolt on the head from Reno."

"Fighting's never stopped you."

"Stopped me what?"

She couldn't say what she meant: loving. Or ask the question she wanted answered: Don't you love me any more?

She put her hand on Zen's. His lay on the table like a big brown fallen leaf, unmoving. The leaf was dead. It had left the tree and its life-giving sap.

The sun, which hadn't cleared the horizon when she arrived, was up now. What had she accomplished by coming over? Drank a cup of coffee with Zen McManus? Touched his hand? And by doing so lessened the possibilities of her ever doing so again.

Walk Memory
1917

11

If Neddie had been more of a talker, his use of dirty words would have been less noticeable. But when, out of a vocabulary of perhaps fifty words, four of the words, with the exception of taking the name of the Lord in vain, were the worst possible, Birdeen was upset. What had come over the boy? Where had he found them? Not at home: "darn" and "consarn it" were as far as she and Reno ever went. Not in any schoolbook. No one in *The Sunbonnet Girls* or *The Overall Boys* used language of that kind. The only explanation must be some foul-mouthed eighth grader, likely in my class, a boy who prided himself on showing younger kids how much more he knew than they did.

Birdeen was set on stopping it. There was only a hair's-breadth of difference between the dirty word in the mouth and the dirty deed in action. Saying the word was a kind of rehearsal. Did anyone ever perform an act for which he didn't have the word? Common sense told Birdeen yes, but didn't convince her that you weren't safer—and certainly nicer—if you were clean-speaking.

There was no use talking to Reno about it. A few dirty words, according to his lights, were as much a part of a boy's growing up as pimples and whiskers. Take him, for example. In his family, he had known such words by the time he was six. Far from preparing him for dirty acts, they had protected him. "Shit" and "piss" didn't make his heart beat any faster than "plow" and "hoe."

This was Chalmers talk, though Reno, by the grace of God and maybe through some help from Birdeen, had escaped the need most Chalmerses had to match their vulgar talk with vulgar acts.

If she went to Reno with an account of what she had heard Neddie say, Reno would have laughed and replied, "The boy's growing up."

So she came to me. I was just as determined as she was to be a nice talker, and to see that Neddie and Ramona were, too. Ramona's vocabulary wasn't bothering anyone yet; but Neddie, for all his quietness, was a boy with a special need, because of his curly hair and plumpness, to prove that he was as tough as any skinny boy with straight hair.

Birdeen, when I came home from school, gave me a glass of milk and a cookie and put me in a rocker. I knew at once that something was wrong. The usual after-school procedure was school clothes off, then help with the housework until suppertime. Fourteen, and larger than my mother, with nothing but a day of sitting at a desk and reading books hidden behind my arithmetic and geography, made a little brisk sweeping and mopping a pleasure.

"Ginerva," Birdeen said, "something bad has happened."

I already knew that. All I wondered was what.

"Neddie is saying bad words."

This *was* news. But I had enough Chalmers blood in my veins to know a bad word wasn't the end of the world. Particularly with Neddie. Neddie, with his dimples and fat stomach, *had* to say "belly" and "butt" and "shit" and "puke" now and then just to prove that, however he looked, he wasn't anybody's apple dumpling.

"I'm not going to tell you what Neddie said," my mother told me.

On the verge of saying "I already know," I swallowed the words. No use upsetting Birdeen any more. There was no danger that she would ever use such words.

"The thing I want to know," she asked, "is where Neddie is picking up language like this."

"Pete Finney."

"Oh, no," Birdeen said. "Peter's mother will be so shamefaced. How do you know it's Peter?"

"Everybody knows."

"Ginerva, Peter is in your class. Now, as Neddie's older sister, you are your brother's keeper. I want you to tell this Finney boy that he must never again use language like that to your little brother."

"What if he says, 'Try and make me'?"

"Tell him you will never speak to him again if he doesn't stop."

I drank the last of my milk, brushed the last cookie crumb from my lips. And rocked. I knew exactly what Pete Finney's reply to that would be. "Can't use dirty words no more or Ginny Chalmers won't talk to me." Then he would screech like a wild man, blubber make-believe tears, and scream once more. "Oh, Ginny, please speak to me." And the kids would laugh their fool heads off.

I didn't tell my mother any of this. Neddie was

proving to be a rougher child than Birdeen had any idea. No use upsetting her with the knowledge that her daughter couldn't stop dirty talking by threatening not to talk to the offender.

"I'll do what I can, Mama."

I didn't have the least intention of telling Pete Finney that I would never speak to him again if he continued to use dirty words to Neddie. Fat lot he would care. If I were a boy, I could do more than threaten him. Pete was about the size of an overgrown grasshopper, and except that a fighting girl was even worse than a dirty-talking boy, I could have shut him up forever with one hard punch.

What I intended to do was to reason with him; and, if he proved reasonable, pray for him. He didn't care a whit, I knew, whether I ever spoke to him again. But he wasn't so far gone, surely, that he didn't care whether or not God abandoned him.

I waited for Pete after school out by the bicycle rack. It was a day of the kind California makes best: September heat finished and October glitter with no hint yet of winter rain, the kind of day summer had been busy preparing and winter was not yet able to touch.

What if I just got on a bike and pedaled away? I didn't own a bike; a bike was a rich kid's plaything. But I could ride. Dell O'Dell had let me learn on his. What if I rode away, skinned down to Zen's garage and said, "I've mastered bikes. Now it's time for cars"?

What if I then drove away and was never heard of

again? Would Neddie go to the dogs if I did that? Would Pete lose his chance to reform and make his peace with God? Was this one of those hinges of history where, for the want of a nail in the shoe of a horse that carried a general, an empire was lost?

There was no way of knowing. All I could do was to stay and do what seemed to be right.

While I was waiting and speculating, Dell O'Dell came out to get his bike.

"Hi, Ginny. You want a ride home?"

"I'm waiting for Pete."

"May be a long wait. He had to stay after class."

"I can wait."

"Didn't know you had a crush on old Pete."

"Maybe I will crush him."

"What's he done?"

"He's teaching Neddie bad words."

"How'd you know?"

"Neddie said so."

"Like what?"

You couldn't get very mad at Dell. Though he was still only half saved, and never prayed or testified, he went to church and Christian Endeavor. He smiled now to let me know his question was a joke. He knew I was never going to repeat what Pete had said to Neddie. He didn't want me to. He really was at least half saved.

Pete, with his sneakers' silent tread, was at our elbow before we saw him. "What you two cooking up?" he asked.

"It's already cooked," I told him.

"Give me a slice."

"Stop teaching Neddie dirty words."

"Like what?"

"You know."

" 'Holy Moses'?"

"No."

" 'Drat it'? 'Doggone it'?"

" 'Shit,' " I yelled, "and you know it."

"Listen to a dirty-talking girl," Pete said to those at the bicycle stand.

"She don't know no dirty words," said Henry Campbell, a fellow Christian Endeavoree.

"Want to bet?" asked Pete.

"No sense betting with someone who ain't got money."

"Bet Dell O'Dell. He's got money."

"I never heard a word," said Dell.

" 'Shit,' " yelled Peter. "You're a liar. 'Shit' is what she said. She teaches her own little brother dirty words. 'Shit. Shit.' Now she's working on me. 'Shit, shit' is what she yelled at me."

I would have tackled anyone, no matter what his size, who said that: Dell O'Dell, broad as a bale of hay, Danny Sievers, tall as a mustard stalk. Swatting a grasshopper like Pete wasn't fair, but in love and war, there are no official rules, and this was both: love for Neddie and war on anyone who tried to make him a dirty talker.

Pete's nose, like the rest of his body, was long and thin, an easy target. I flattened it. Blood spattered from it like water from an artesian well.

"You struck a gusher," Henry yelled. "Ten thousand barrels a day."

Pete was gushing, all right, but he had plenty of blood, and the loss of a gallon or two didn't slow him down. He came at me like an enraged tarantula, small but vicious. He snatched at my hair, clawed at my face with his fingernails, even snapped his teeth at me when I got within biting distance.

Both halves of Dell O'Dell, the saved and the unsaved, knew what to do: the unsaved would take care of Pete the fighter, the saved would rejoice in protecting me and in accepting my appreciation.

Pete was a wisp to handle, though messy with blood. There wasn't much point in smashing him any more. Dell picked him up, set him astraddle Pete's own bicycle, put his hands on the handlebars, and gave him a good shove down the slope that led from the school to the road.

Pete kept going; no one expected him to return. I might not be able to lick him permanently, but Dell O'Dell could, and add more to the gusher's output if he came back.

Dell felt sorry for me. Maybe he felt something more. I thought so, and I liked the thought, even if I could hardly admit it. It seemed I was always, with the best intentions in the world, getting myself into trouble. Take that time I made him switch my legs. I didn't get into any trouble with that, but if I'd asked some other boy to do the switching, legs might have been just the beginning for him.

And yelling "shit" now, to a kid I was trying to stop talking dirty to my little brother. That didn't make sense.

Dell knew I was far from crazy. I could beat everyone in our class—not the way I had Pete, but get better grades. The trouble was, I didn't see the same world everyone else saw. I was a mess now: scratches on my face, hair unbraided, as much blood on me as if I'd been the gusher.

"Want me to ride you home?"

"I look pretty awful, don't I?"

"We can stop at the Anaheim Ditch, and you can wash up."

The Anaheim Ditch was Valencia's big irrigation canal, the nearest we had to a river. It was drinking water as well as irrigation water, and kids weren't supposed to swim in it or let cats drown in it. They did both, though the Mexican who patrolled the ditch with his two-wheeled cart fished both out, alive or dead.

"I'll stop at the bridge," Dell said.

"No one would ever know you'd been in a fracas now," Dell said when I'd finished washing and combing.

In a waterless land, the ditch, with its cattails and wild tobacco plants, was as sweet as an oasis with palm trees. Nothing dead floated by. The Mexican and his two-wheeled cart were nowhere to be seen.

"You lied about not hearing what I said," I told Dell.

Was this going to be another do-what's-right-and-switch my-legs day? Go tell Pete that he *did* hear me yelling "shit"? Well, he wouldn't do it.

"But in love and war, all's fair," I added. Dell didn't

ask which this was, and he didn't have to. "This was war against wrong," I said.

"So what I said was all right."

"It was fair. We had to stop Pete."

"He's stopped."

"Some ways I'm just as bad as Pete. I said his bad word and then I hit him."

"Pete didn't *hit* anybody. But what you said was just a slang word to Pete."

"Slang? Like 'beat it'? Or 'tell your old man'?"

"No. Real bad. Like where babies come from."

"There's nothing bad about that. Neddie and I have known that for years."

"How'd you find out?"

"Mama told us."

"What did she tell you?"

"You know. God places a seed in a woman, and it grows and grows, and in nine months the seed is a full-sized baby."

"Where does it grow?"

"In a woman's stomach. Then, in nine months, it comes out of a place that opens up so the baby can be born. That's why widows and old maids don't have babies. Just wives and husbands, so the husband can earn the money to take care of the baby. There's nothing dirty about that. Mama wouldn't have told us if there was."

"That ain't the way Pete tells it."

"There's no way anybody can make God's work dirty."

"Pete can make it *sound* dirty."

"I don't see how."

"Don't girls ever talk to you about babies?"

"Not when I tell them I already know all there is to know."

"Then they shut up?"

"If they don't, I walk away. Mama told me to. She knows more about it than they do. They never had any babies."

"So what do you think Pete said to Neddie?"

"You know what he said. You heard me yell it."

"I sure did."

"Mama just expected me to shut Pete up. Not spend the rest of the day talking about him."

"Suits me. What'll we talk about?"

"Water."

"The ditch?"

"The ocean. Why does it scare me?"

"It's over your head. You don't like to be in over your head."

"Well, who does?"

"Swimmers do."

"I'm learning. I can backstroke already."

Dell pretended he was testing the muscle of my upper arm. "Poor Pete," he said. "No wonder he gushed."

"You think I'm strong?"

"In this arm," said Dell, and tested the other arm. "Strong here, too."

"Do you like strong girls?"

"Not if they swat me."

"I won't ever swat you, Dell O'Dell."

Dell, a hand on each arm, was in a position to give me a good hug. He did so.

I was surprised to feel tears slipping down my cheeks.

"Did I hurt you, Ginny?"

"No. Nobody ever hugged me before."

"Not your folks?"

"They hug each other, not us kids."

"What made you cry?"

"It was so unexpected. Like a Christmas present you never thought you'd receive."

"If hugging's Christmas, we don't have to wait 'til December."

"Christmas every month would spoil it."

"I guess you're right."

On the bicycle once again, Dell said, "Next time Pete tries any dirty talk on Neddie, let me handle him."

"I will. You're really three-quarters saved, Dell O'Dell."

12

California, according to Easterners, doesn't have much weather. No seasons, no blizzards, no thunderstorms, no twisters, no hurricanes. Not even snow.

Southern California does have that dry little wind off the desert they call the Santa Ana. The Santa Ana never pushed over anything bigger than a tumbleweed; never sent anything flying heavier than loose sand or a eucalyptus pod. Thus Californians are without much to talk about in the way of weather. There *is* rain: early, late, or nonexistent. In the arroyos of the dry foothills, there *is* an occasional flash flood.

There was, or there once had been, an earthquake in California, though not in Southern California. All Southern California had was earthquake weather. Salubrious Valencia had almost more earthquake weather than any other part of the state. Constant sunshine, an annual eight inches of rain, with nothing ever more disturbing than an occasional Santa Ana or flash flood, earthquake weather was almost the only weather there was to talk about. There was no record of any accurate foretelling of an earthquake by earthquake weather. But everyone felt that after some such day, at some future time, *the* earthquake would come.

Let a day be overcast but warm, muggy but rainless, leaves motionless, sounds carrying unusual distances in the quiet, then everyone believed that unusual and probably dangerous weather was being prepared. For Easterners, such warnings might foretell thunderstorms or twisters. In California, no little turmoils of wind or rain were expected. Instead, a movement of earth itself, a real shaker, earth threatening to fall apart, to have crevasses wrenched open, deep enough to swallow the whole of Valencia; or possibly strong enough to unanchor earth from its accustomed place between sun and moon and send it wandering, sunless and moonless, into uncharted space.

It might happen. California wasn't any carbon copy of Iowa or Indiana. Valencia residents hadn't traveled two thousand miles for the sake of getting more of the same. California products were all bigger, usually better, than those they had back East.

Earthquake weather affected people in two different ways. Some thought that it was useless in the face of impending disaster to pay the bills, wash the dishes, or milk the cows. Others, like Birdeen, relished hurdles to leap. Even hurdles as big as threatened earthquakes. If her house was going to be tumbled down a crevasse or cracked like a piece of peanut brittle, let it go clean and tidy.

Taking the dust of the last Santa Ana off the front windows, Birdeen didn't notice Zen drive in the side driveway.

"I see you're getting ready for the quake," he said.

"You don't believe that talk, do you?" If he did, she was glad to see that he didn't believe in stopping work until the jolt was over.

"No. California's yelled wolf too often for me to think earthquakes and weather have any connection."

"What're you doing away from the office?"

"Garage."

"Garage?"

"Took a lady for a test drive."

"Can't she drive?"

"Sure, but with me along, it's an outing—and a sale, I hope."

"Ginerva says she's taking test driving. Don't you think she's a little young for test drives?"

"She's fourteen. She can have a car at sixteen."

"You planning on giving her one?"

"Rate she's coming along, I might do that."

"Come on in. In time of earthquake, they say, stay away from glass windows."

"Got any coffee left over from breakfast? In time of earthquake, they say, keep up your strength."

Zen sprawled himself out on the wicker rocker on the front porch. "No use going inside in weather like this."

Birdeen handed Zen the Valencia *Star,* a weekly paper that had come the day before. "Read this while I get the coffee."

Much of the first two pages carried summaries of the campaigns in Europe. President Wilson was quoted on the progress of American troops fighting in France. Perhaps it was the overwhelming seriousness of the conflict, or the difficulty of understanding bewildering facts and staggering figures, or the realization of a threat that could reach out six thousand miles from strange, unheard-of places—perhaps all of these caused the people of Valencia to discuss the war solemnly in the still hours after the children were asleep. This was not earthquake weather, worthy of an ironic joke. This was carnage, deserving of mortal concern.

When she returned, coffee for him, Congoin, the tropical tea, for her, she said, "Well, what do you think?"

"I think there are too many used cars on the market."

"Zen, you haven't even read the paper."

"I read the used-car ads. What did you have in mind?"

Birdeen, from her twin rocker, took the *Star* from Zen, folded it open to the third page, then handed it back.

"Read that," she said.

"'Second Reservoir for Valencia.' That it?"

Why was she willing to put up with so much more nonsense from Zen than she would from Reno? She didn't love Zen more than Reno. But there was a difference between what you expected from a brother and from a husband. Besides, Reno didn't have the Chalmers turn to be funny. If he had asked that question, he would have meant it.

"Not the reservoir. The new movie theater, 'The Rialto.'"

"Birdie, I never knew you were so crazy about movies."

Even brothers could carry joking too far. "Not the movie. The contest they are having. Read that."

"Fifty-dollar prize! Rialto Theater offers a fifty-dollar prize opening day for the best imitation of Charlie Chaplin. Contest to take place on the main street of Valencia between two and three on the afternoon of the opening of the Rialto Theater."

"That it?" Zen asked when he finished reading.

Birdeen nodded.

135

"You planning on entering?"

"I recite; I don't act. Besides, I'm not funny."

"You got somebody in mind who is? Me?"

"You're funny, all right, but you can't act."

"Reno's no contender."

"Ginerva."

"You're out of your mind."

"No, I'm not. You ought to see Ginny here at home. We laugh our heads off at her antics. She likes to make people laugh. She doesn't get stage fright. You saw her at the Temperance contest."

"Have you talked to her about it?"

"Not yet. But I've already paid the five-dollar entrance fee. Ginny isn't the kind of girl to let me spend five dollars for nothing. And she'll win the fifty dollars. I know. And she knows we need it. It's for Neddie's teeth. She'll jump at the chance."

"Got any more coffee?"

"That's the last."

"Too bad. I need it."

"You feeling dauncy?"

"I am, Birdie. I really am. I never thought to see the day when a sister of mine would sell her own daughter."

"Sell? Now you're out of your mind, Zen. I'm giving her the chance to do what she likes to do, and make money at it besides."

"Birdie, Birdie. There's nothing like a woman's mind."

"I guess you ought to know, Zen."

"I know your daughter better than you do. Sure, if you ask her to do it, and for Neddie's teeth in the bargain, she'll do it. But don't you remember when you were fourteen?"

"I wasn't nearly as grown-up as Ginerva when I was fourteen."

"I bet you weren't. You were a wispy little thing like Mama. Ginerva's a young lady. What makes you think she wants to put on baggy pants, have a mustache glued to her upper lip, carry a cane, and wear broken-down outsize shoes? She's just at the age when she wants to look good. Not parade in clown clothes down the middle of the main street to the heehaws of onlookers."

"Charlie Chaplin isn't a clown."

"That outfit of his is a clown suit. How do you expect to squeeze Ginerva into it, anyway? She's no undersized middle-aged man."

"People don't expect her to *be* Charlie Chaplin, just to act more like him than the other contestants."

Birdeen didn't speak to Ginerva about the Rialto contest until after supper almost a week later. Ginerva had given them all a sidesplitting demonstration of a mishap that had befallen their American history teacher. Miss Donaldson, a buxom lady of forty, had worn a full-skirted dress of soft material that day.

They had been studying the Civil War in the afternoon, and to help her class keep the great battles in mind, Miss Donaldson was listing them on the board as the class called out the names to her.

The class loved this exercise. Nothing was required but a good memory.

As the list grew, "Battle of Manassas," "Battle of the

Wilderness," "Missionary Ridge," "Spotsylvania," "Gettysburg," "Battle of Atlanta," Miss Donaldson bent lower and lower to do the necessary writing.

The mishap occurred at "Missionary Ridge." Bending to write those two words, a fold of Miss Donaldson's soft full skirt was somehow caught in the crease between her two ample buttocks. A sight was revealed that the class was never expected to see. Unaware of what had happened, Miss Donaldson, hearing the laughter, turned to discover its cause. Facing them, there was no more laughter. But when she turned to write "Battle of Pine Top," guffawing again filled the room. There was nothing sidesplitting about death and destruction in the War Between the States; there was no accounting for adolescent hysteria, either. Miss Donaldson turned to face a quiet and even shamefaced class. She forgave them.

But she was not a teacher to be trifled with. The heehawing started again before she had written "Battle."

A class that snickered at history at its most bloody was not a class in a mood to learn.

"In the Middle Ages," she told them, "people died of the dancing sickness. You seem to have come down with the giggling germ. I trust that you will have recovered by tomorrow. Meanwhile, I feel that it would be more seemly for you to do your laughing outside the classroom. Class dismissed."

13

I told the whole story at the supper table. First, I was the class heehawing. Then I was Miss Donaldson, writing on the board, angry and flabbergasted, dismissing the class.

Neddie, a practical boy, said, "Show us how her dress went."

I, entrusted with keeping Neddie a nice, clean boy, and feeling a little guilty because of the story I had told, said, "You should be ashamed of yourself, Neddie, for having such thoughts."

"You gave them to me."

Well, I had. I was too modest to demonstrate with my own dress Miss Donaldson's plight; but it was my words that had made Neddie want to see demonstrated what he had heard described.

When supper was over, Birdeen said to Neddie and Ramona, "Now, you two clear the table. I've got some things I want to talk over with Ginerva."

Neddie and Ramona exchanged glances. Big sister was going to get it.

"What's your plan for me?" Reno asked. Nobody had to make plans for Reno on Friday night after supper. He would read the *Star*. He already had it in his hand and was bound for the front porch, his favorite chair, and the last of the daylight.

"Let's go to the sitting room," Birdeen said to me. "That was a pretty funny story, Sister."

139

"I hope I didn't make Miss Donaldson sound vulgar."

"Oh, no. Unlucky."

"Or the kids sound too crazy?"

"No, no. They sounded like kids. And Miss Donaldson like anybody in an embarrassing situation."

"Who didn't know it."

"That's right. When I heard you, I knew I had done the right thing. I hope you think so, too."

"What, Mama?"

"I entered you in the Rialto contest."

"To be Charlie Chaplin? It costs five dollars."

"I've already paid it."

"Charlie doesn't talk."

"I reckon you can hold your tongue for ten or fifteen minutes."

"Charlie is a man."

"That's what'll make it all the funnier. A young girl pretending to be a middle-aged man."

"Papa wouldn't be very funny pretending to be Charlie, would he?"

"He might be funnier than you think. But there's no point worrying about that because he's never going to do it."

"I wouldn't really be pretending to be Charlie."

"I don't know why not."

"I'd just be pretending to be the clown Charlie's pretending to be."

"That's the only Charlie anyone knows."

"In real life, I bet his pants fit and he probably doesn't have any mustache at all."

"Maybe. But the prize is for the best imitation of whoever Charlie's pretending to be."

"Prize?"

"Fifty dollars. Didn't you read the ad? It's just what's needed to straighten Neddie's teeth."

"It wouldn't be the same as imitating Miss Donaldson, would it? Making fun of a real person?"

"Who would want to see that?"

"It was Miss Donaldson's feelings I was thinking of. Trying to make her look funny. I wouldn't want to do that."

"It wouldn't be the same at all."

"Do you think I can do it?"

"I think you could be Teddy Roosevelt if you set your mind to it."

"I'll have to have a costume."

"That's one thing I can do. And if you faint, I'll be right up there, grab your cane and mustache. And take the fifty dollars."

"The way I did the medal."

"Only I won't throw the money away."

Birdeen could make me laugh. No hugging, no kissing. No reading of stories aloud. No shared prayers. But laughing together was a mingling, maybe closer than hugging and kissing; a hugger or kisser, in many cases, might as well have been embracing stone. But the laughter of two laughees really mingles and makes the two one.

By the time the Rialto had its contest, the earthquake weather had produced the earthquake it foretold, a moderate tremor down in Riverside County. The weather in Valencia had become what was normal for inland Southern California in October, dry, clear, and hot.

It wasn't the kind of weather for a Charlie Chaplin outfit. Pants are always hotter than skirts; and, underneath my mustache, beads of sweat were gathering so fast that I was afraid they might loosen the mucilage that held it on.

I had seen Charlie Chaplin only once in a movie. I could make myself look like Charlie, helped by a tight Ferris waist and a rented hat that came equipped with a fringe of black hair. The Ferris flattened me, the mustache made the flatness look manly—but Charlie had something I wasn't able to duplicate. He was sad in the eyes, sad and solemn, thinking of better things. When *he* had mishaps, they shouldn't have made audiences laugh. The class had laughed at Miss Donaldson, but they had been ashamed of themselves for doing so. Charlie *wanted* people to laugh. That's what he was famous for, laughter at a little man who wanted to be admired for his dignity and high-mindedness, and who, try as he would, couldn't avoid ludicrous mishaps. It wasn't the clown they laughed at; it was the little man, Charlie himself, who wore the clown suit. Clowns are supposed to be funny. They work at it. And nothing is funny that has to be worked at. You can't laugh at a man who provides his own banana peels for slipping.

It was the man inside the suit that the girl inside the Ferris waist was afraid she could not be. No one would win the prize by throwing out banana peels for his own downfall. That was the magic part of funniness. The banana peel had to appear to be thrown by someone else.

It wouldn't have been funny if Miss Donaldson had tucked her skirt between her buttocks herself. That would have been vulgar, not funny.

If sidesplitting things happened only to those who loved dignity and the world's solemn beauty, how could I, entered in a contest to make money, make anyone laugh?

No matter what happened to Charlie, you knew that he, dignified and beauty-loving, was the victim. I could dress like Charlie and walk like Charlie and twirl my cane like Charlie; but I didn't know how to be a victim.

Birdeen had my Charlie Chaplin outfit ready a week before the contest. She thought that I would need a week, at least, to get used to wearing pants, having a mustache, and twirling a cane.

I learned fast. I looked like Charlie, all right, except for the sad eyes. I tried out my costume on Neddie.

"What you wearing men's clothes for?" Neddie asked.

"I'm pretending to be a man."

"Why?" Neddie asked.

"It's a contest. The one who looks most like a man wins."

"Are men in the contest?"

"If they want to be."

"They'll win."

"You have to be funny."

"Why?"

"It's the contest."

"Your mustache is funny. It looks like string."

"It's human hair. Mostly the contest is what you do, not how you look."

"What're you going to do?"

"I'm going to act like Charlie Chaplin. You don't go to movies, Neddie. You don't know anything about Charlie Chaplin."

"I went to a movie once."

"Who did you see?"

"I saw Ben Turpin. He was funny. He was cross-eyed."

"What did he *do*?"

"He chased a duck."

I stared at my brother. The Romans told fortunes by the shape of the entrails of animals. Fate gave me a little brother who could foretell the future. Aunt Cissie had a pet duck. If chasing a duck was funny, I could do that.

Neddie, for all of his ability to foretell the future, wasn't able to foretell the fact that the duck would teach me to be a victim, which was what a comedian has to learn to be.

14

Zen gave me driving lessons on Saturday mornings. Auto selling wasn't booming at that time at the garage. He had heard about the Rialto contest and disapproved of it. But until the day before the contest he had never seen me manly and flattened in my Ferris waist and hairy and comic in my false mustache. What he saw didn't cause him to change his opinion.

"My God in heaven," he said, "what have they done to you, Aunt Jetty?"

"Don't you recognize me, Uncle Zen?"

"Sure, I recognize you. You're my schoolgirl niece all decked out to make a public fool of herself."

Birdeen loved Zen, but he was carrying things too far by undermining my confidence.

"You'll be the only one there who doesn't recognize Charlie Chaplin when they see him. Or laugh their heads off when his duck starts a parade of its own."

"Duck! What duck?"

"It's under a tub on the back porch now."

"Charlie Chaplin never had a duck."

"Ben Turpin did. It was sidesplitting."

"Does Ginerva have to cross her eyes, too?"

"Now, Zen, for a man who's done the fool things you've done, it don't sit well with me to hear you downgrade your own flesh and blood."

"Aunt Jetty, do you want to do this?"

"Yes, I do, Uncle Zen."

"O.K. Change your clothes and we'll have our driving lesson."

"She's wearing them so she'll feel natural in them tomorrow," Birdeen said.

"I won't feel natural giving a driving lesson to a man with a duck."

"The duck isn't going. He spatters."

"Maybe you'd better get used to that, too."

"I could skip this week's lesson."

"Let's not skip this lesson, Aunt Jetty. Keep that suit on. Cross your eyes if you want to. Take the duck, too. He's likely got more driving sense than some customers I've had."

"It's a she."

"No doubt about the sense, then."

Actually, there was no need of more lessons. I could drive as well as Zen could. He knew it and he had an idea that I knew it. If I did know it, why didn't I say, "Thanks, Uncle Zen, but you don't need to waste any more time on me"?

The answer to that, the only answer there could be, was that I enjoyed the rides. I didn't want them to end.

He didn't, either. The only reason for continuing them that would be acceptable to Birdeen and Reno would be what he had promised me—a new car with some kind of different shift. Sixteen was still some months off.

"If I was dressed as a woman, with false curls and a padded-out front, would you mind driving down the main street of Valencia with me?"

"No."

"I'd look like a fool, you know. A man pretending to be a woman."

"I'd know you were a man."

"How?"

"You're an uncle."

Zen threw an arm across my shoulders. I was too good a driver to be disturbed by such suddenness.

"So I am. And you're an aunt. No matter what we're wearing."

"I don't care what people think. Do you?"

"Not a smidgin."

"What's a smidgin?"

"Back-East talk. That's what we said instead of 'not a whit,' back there."

"What's a 'whit'?"

"A big smidgin."

"Teach me back-East talk, Uncle Zen. You taught me a lot of things."

"Yes, I did."

"Reading."

"What was the first?"

"To walk through the woods without getting scared."

"Oh, Aunt Jetty, you were a little sweetheart to do that for me."

"Give me her glasses. I'll be Love."

Zen whipped the glasses out and settled them on my nose. Then he kissed me.

"First time I ever kissed anybody with a mustache."

I pulled the mustache off.

"Now I'm Love, not Charlie."

"You're still a driver, though. Better take the glasses off, too."

"Her glasses fit me. I can see anything she saw."

15

The contest began at 2:30 P.M. That gave everyone time to go to church, go home for dinner, then change from church clothes into parade clothes. Half the town appeared to be rigged out as Charlie; the other half was there to watch that half make fools of themselves.

Zen was to drive Ginerva to the point where female Charlies were to assemble for marching. This left Reno, Birdeen, and the kids free to shift for themselves, go early and find the best parking space available.

Temporary grandstands had been erected, and seats were free for those who had bought tickets for that night's show at the Rialto.

Everyone thought that it would have been much more appropriate for the Rialto owner to have chosen a Chaplin movie for his premiere opening, rather than Richard Barthelmess. But the Rialto owner knew his business. Chaplin was a man as well known as Santa Claus or Uncle Sam. Who wouldn't enjoy seeing him imitated? But who would want to see the real Charlie after viewing scores of masqueraders?

Birdeen and Reno had already left when Zen arrived. To him, every iota of Ginerva Chalmers was drained from her being as she came down the steps, hat atilt, mustache solid, cane twirling. Even the duck who rode on her shoulder was the bird of a dapper little man whose goal was dignity in spite of it.

Zen had enough sense not to say, "Good morning,

Charlie." She was the one who was playacting, not he.

"What's the duck's name?" he asked.

"Duck."

"I should have known. Henny-penny. Turkey-lurkey."

"I didn't name her."

The spell was broken. She was not Charlie. She was a girl dressed like Charlie with a duck that belonged to an aunt.

"What have they done to the town?"

"Decorated it."

"It looks like Decoration Day. Or the Fourth of July."

"Does it make you nervous?"

"I'd feel better if I could talk."

"Charlie doesn't."

"I know. But the camera came up so close to him, people could see into his eyes."

"What was there?"

"A victim."

"Not much victim in you."

"The duck will make me one."

"How'd you figure that out?"

"Neddie told me. He saw a duck make a victim out of Ben Turpin."

"Then people will laugh?"

"Yes. It will be funnier with Charlie. He is dressed like a snob."

"You don't look very snobbish to me."

"It's my cane and mustache. I'm putting on the dog. Then, when I have my comeuppance, people will laugh."

"You sure you want to go through with this?"

"No. Give me the glasses. I'd rather be Love than Charlie. She never made anyone laugh, did she?"

"She never made me laugh, Aunt Jetty. Never made fifty dollars, either. She was a real victim."

"She died, though. I'm not going to die. I'm going to make people laugh and make money. And win a medal."

Zen, who could drive with one hand, leaned over and kissed his niece. No word about false mustaches now, or victim hidden deep in the eyes of a famous comedian.

"Little sweetheart, you'll do it. I guarantee it."

Zen took Ginerva to where the parade was to start, at the elementary school building on Avocado Street. Then he found himself a good parking spot on Guava. The contestants would walk, march, run, whatever they elected to do, six blocks down Avocado, then make a right turn onto Guava for a final six blocks to the Methodist church and the judges' grandstand.

Zen had as good a view of the proceedings from the top of his coupe as anyone who had a seat as a result of buying a ticket to the Rialto show that evening. In addition to providing himself with a view, his car was advertising the fact that his motor company had the only new-model Hupmobile in town.

He was noticed. New car or old, there were no other cars with their owners on top of them. Sarah Loomis would probably have seen him if he had been sitting on the curb. For what other reason had she come to this ridiculous parade? For a glimpse only, without any hope that she would find him planted as conspicuously as a lighthouse above a wash of look-alike water.

She waved and called. Not knowing that Zen was advertising a line of cars as well as watching a parade, Zen's invitation to join him amazed her.

"Up there?"

"Sure. Where else?"

She was not built like a climber, but she was sturdy and the Hup was sturdy, and, with Zen's help for the last clamber, she made it from hubcap to fender to hood to the top.

"This is the last place I expected to see you, Zen."

He was too tactful to say, "What brings you here, then?" He said, "I brought my niece over. She's in it."

"I've seen you with her several times recently."

"I'm teaching her to drive."

"What do you think of her parading around like a man?"

"I don't think she'll fool anybody."

"Who put her up to it? Birdeen?"

"Likely."

"It's a charade. But isn't the whole of life a charade? We all want to be someone else. Go to church and swallow bread and wine and think we're Jesus Christ Himself as a result. I sit with you here, your lady friend to all appearances. Just as false as any of the Charlie Chaplins. I'm neither a lady nor your friend. What happened, Zen?"

"As far as I'm concerned, you're still a lady and a friend."

"Hell, Zen. You didn't want either in the beginning

and whatever you want now, what you've got is something else. When's this parade going to start?"

"It's starting," said Zen.

Over on Avocado, a bugle sounded.

"Sounds like a horse race," said Sarah.

Whatever it was, the audience on Avocado liked it. Their laughter could be plainly heard on Guava. The parade, in honor of a man who had built a career on exposing life's vagaries, had been organized by men who were doing their best to correct this flaw.

The line-up of contestants was orderly. No effort had been made to separate men from women. Half of the fun was the inability to tell one from the other. Age groups had been recognized: children, young people, adults. It was unfair for grownups, that is, anyone over fourteen, to have to compete with a nine-year-old Charlie of any sex.

Neddie's belief that funniness was hinged upon doing, not being, was borne out by the contestants. They pushed wheelbarrows, rode hobby-horses, led dogs, ate pies that dribbled.

No one else had a duck. Perhaps there was no other duck in existence like Ginerva's. Sarah had expected Ginerva, who was a pretty girl, to attract attention. She hadn't expected her to be a star. Was she going to resent every female, even someone young enough to be Zen's daughter? If she saw Zen give Birdeen a good-bye clasp and kiss, would her blood boil? Just because Zen didn't want to kiss *her* any more didn't mean that he had given up kissing. And what did it matter, as far as she was concerned? Kith and kin or a total stranger?

As the young people's group, close on the heels of the kids, came around the corner onto Guava, Ginerva's duck, who had been riding sedately on her shoulder, spied a better means of transportation. She flew into the wheelbarrow pushed by a stout Charlie, Sam Tyson, son of the owner of Tyson's Dry Goods Store.

Charlie—Ginerva's Charlie—was not a man to take insubordination from a duck. Without hesitation and without ceasing to be a dandy with a cane and a hard black hat, she high-stepped to the wheelbarrow. There, not touching the bird but with some inaudible but patently authoritative words, she issued orders. Duck left the wheelbarrow to perch again, not on her shoulder, but on her hat.

There was laughter and hearty applause as she regained her place in the line of march. Duck showed his appreciation of the applause. On the top of Charlie's black hat, she spattered. Nothing overdone; but what she did was visible.

Ginerva couldn't see what had happened, but the crowd's whoops told her. Now she had become a real victim and was really funny. She took the duck from her hat, and the hat from her head. Out of her pocket she pulled no farmer's red bandanna, but a dandy's white square. With it, she mopped first the hat, then the duck. Finally, hat back on head, she set the duck at her feet. With a sharp rap of her cane, which Duck seemed to understand, she set her to walking the parade route without benefit of a shoulder to rest on or a wheelbarrow.

People in the grandstand rose to their feet and clapped.

They had been given a victim; and something more humiliating than a slippery banana peel. Funnier, too. Shit on the hero's hat.

"What do you think of that?" Sarah asked. What she thought was, a girl would need a lot of brass to be willing to make a public spectacle of herself in that way. Have to be pretty sure in the first place of her attractiveness to dress like a clown and consort with a duck. Or perhaps know that she was valued for qualities that false mustaches and dirty ducks could not disguise.

"I envy her," Sarah said. "I could never have done anything like that. I would have cried if a duck had done that on my head. What kept *her* from crying?"

"She was Charlie Chaplin. She was doing what he would do. He wasn't a kid."

"You like that?"

"Sure. I like people who do what they set out to do."

"It didn't work with me."

"No?"

"I set out to be your wife. That didn't make you like me."

"Sure it did, Sarah. I like you. I don't marry everyone I like. And I married one, at least, I didn't like. Let's go to the judges' stand."

"You'd rather see if your niece won a medal than hear about my broken heart."

"Sarah, you're a mind reader."

Most of the contestants had accepted the fact that they weren't winners. And no one was surprised when Judge Jessup asked Ginerva to step forward.

"The first prize," said he, "goes to Ginerva Chalmers and her duck. Ginerva was the perfect Charlie and her duck was the perfect laugh-getter. Since the purpose of this contest was laughs, the medal goes by rights to the duck."

Walk Memory
1919

16

Dell O'Dell was the janitor at the post office. He was young for the job, seventeen, but not small: five eleven and one hundred and seventy-five pounds. He did odd jobs for Sarah, as well as the routine post-office sweeping and window washing. So he wasn't surprised when Sarah told him she would need him for an extra day in the last week of August.

"You come early tomorrow," she told him when he left the post office Friday evening, "and I'll let you know what I have in mind."

He came early, and a good thing. What Sarah had in mind wasn't janitorial and required considerable explaining.

"Can you ride a bicycle, Dell?"

A boy of seventeen who couldn't ride a bicycle was maimed. That was as ridiculous a question as if she had asked if he could walk.

"Since I was six."

"I don't care about how long. How well is more to the point."

Dell thought, but didn't ask, Is racing what you have in mind?

Maybe Sarah could read his mind. "What I had in mind," she said, "would require some ability."

"I got some," Dell said.

"You're a friend of Ginerva Chalmers, aren't you?"

"We're in the same class."

"I'm going to share in giving a birthday party for Ginerva. I'll need some help."

"Me and my bike," Dell said. "Tell me when."

"We won't need your bike," Sarah said.

Dell said nothing. What all the bike talk had been about, he didn't know.

"Ginerva's folks are having a party for her."

"I'm invited," Dell told Sarah.

"Then you know all about it," Sarah said.

"All I know is that when Ginny is sixteen, her folks are giving her a party and I'm invited."

"That's about the sum of it," Sarah said. "Except that I would like it to be a more suitable party."

"Suitable," Dell said, trying to think of something unsuitable Reno and Birdeen might plan for a party for their daughter. Because of Birdeen, there wouldn't be anything unsuitable in the way of drinking or card playing. Reno, who didn't dance himself, thought the hugging and hopping of entwined men and women less suitable than conversation or charades. Dell didn't feel bold enough to ask Sarah Loomis a point-blank question such as, "Unsuitable in what way, Miss Loomis?" After all, he was invited and would know in what his mother called "good time" what was unsuitable about the planned party.

He didn't have to wait for "good time."

"In my opinion," said Sarah, "it would be more suitable if guests celebrating the birthday of a sixteen-year-old were somewhere near her own age."

"I'm near," said Dell.

"There should be others."

"You could ask them."

"I have asked them. That's why I need you."

"And my bike," Dell said, the first ray of light illuminating the bike situation.

"No," said Sarah. "My bike."

Dell didn't know that Sarah had a bike. He had never seen her on one, and if she had one, couldn't imagine her pedaling away on it. But if she had one, and could pedal, what part could it play in a birthday party for a sixteen-year-old?

Maybe it was an antique? The first bicycle ever seen west of the Rockies? Miss Loomis had received it on her sixteenth birthday and now was passing it on to another sixteener?

That wasn't too crazy. But it didn't do anything to explain the reason he and his bike were mixed up with Sarah's bike, or Ginerva's birthday party.

"I bet you're wondering why I need you."

"Yeh," Dell said, "I am."

"To present the gift."

"What gift?"

"The bike."

"My bike?"

"No, not yours. Mine."

"I didn't know you had one."

"I don't. I've bought one as a gift for the birthday girl. Five speeds. And since this is going to be a party with lots of young people, I'm not the one to come wheeling a new bicycle. You are."

Dell saw at once that he could do the job more appropriately than Sarah.

"The gift would be yours," he said. "I'd just be the delivery boy."

"You could keep it over at your house 'til the party, couldn't you?"

"Sure," Dell said. "There wouldn't be any riding of it. I can guarantee that."

When asked about the new bicycle, Dell explained by the word "storage." Even after Sarah had explained to him her own ideas as to what would follow "storage."

On the day of the party, after the games and before the refreshments, Sarah would announce her own gift of appreciation and congratulation to Ginerva, who had been her year-long help in the distribution of the mail.

After her announcement, in would come Dell, astride the bicycle, wearing a delivery boy's jacket and cap made by Sarah as appropriate for the occasion. Dell wasn't averse to the idea. It was as near as he would ever get to being a Kentucky Derby jockey. That bicycle would never move so fast again; he'd guarantee that, and he wouldn't want it to. Number One run should be for Ginerva.

17

I knew about the birthday party, of course. I had known about Zen's gift since I had known there *were* birthday parties. When I was sixteen, if I had learned to drive, he would give me an automobile. By this time I even knew what I couldn't have known earlier: the make of the car, the color, the upholstery. I had seen the car. It was down at Zen's garage, and anybody in town who was curious about what Zen was giving his niece for her birthday could stop in and have a look.

I did. And, as Zen said, people got double their money's worth. Niece and car together. The car was a Hup, of course, since that was what Zen sold.

I knew as much about Birdeen's plans and Zen's gift to me as I knew little about Sarah Loomis's part in it. All I knew about it was that the kids of my class were going to be there and that Dell O'Dell was helping Miss Loomis prepare for it.

That was all I wanted to know about it. I didn't try to wheedle a bit more out of Dell, though I could tell that he wanted to be wheedled. He knew something that he thought would make my birthday the best ever if I only knew. But I wouldn't ask him, and rather than burst with the untold information, he blurted it all forth without the least bit of encouragement from me. It was tell or pop, and he chose to tell.

When he had revealed the big news to me and had seen how little I was impressed with a five-speed bike on the day I was receiving an eight-cylinder Hupmobile, he wished he had kept his mouth shut. It was too late for that. A bicycle was a ridiculous gift to put up in competition with an automobile. A book, a bottle of cologne, a box of candy, something that didn't suggest comparisons at all—that would make sense.

Dell saw this afterward, because he talked about it to Birdeen and she talked to me.

"Poor Dell O'Dell," she said. "He told me."

I knew that something was amiss when the usual cookie, glass of milk, and rocking chair were offered me when I got home from school.

Mama just rocked, in her chair. "Dell thought people might believe Miss Loomis was trying to outdo Uncle Zen. And that you wanted her to and were trying to help her."

"Uncle Zen is giving me a car. How can Miss Loomis outdo that?"

"I didn't say she could. Actually, it was Dell who said it, that people might think it."

"Why would they?"

I knew why they would. And it wasn't anything I wanted to talk about with Birdeen. Or anybody.

"Zen's reputation is well known around here. The person you better try to figure out is Dell."

"Have you?"

"I think I understand the trouble he's in now."

"Trouble? What trouble?"

"He told you Miss Loomis's secret."

"The bicycle? I never asked him."

"That makes it worse for him. She asked him not to

tell, and the first thing he does is to tell you. The second thing he does is to tell me. I admit he was asking for advice. He was ashamed of breaking his word to Miss Loomis. I told him not to worry about Miss Loomis. She was perfectly willing to have him look like a fool as he came pedaling in on her bicycle following Zen in his Hup. And Zen himself won't look too smart showing off in competition with a bicycle rider."

"She wouldn't do that. She wants Uncle Zen to be her beau."

"Zen will never guess it when he sees himself imitated by a kid on a bicycle."

I don't think Zen cared what a kid on a bicycle did. Or what Sarah Loomis wanted of *him*. Or cared what people thought *he* wanted. Not after they'd had a look at the yellow Hup with the red leather upholstery. If they could buy a car like that to give to a kid, they wouldn't care what people thought.

That was my reasoning, anyway. So I talked to Dell, not Zen, about the party.

Dell didn't know about the Hup. I might have been talking to Neddie. Only the saved part of Dell seemed to have any idea of what had been going on. And that part saw only goodness in Miss Loomis. She wouldn't want him to act like an idiot; she wouldn't want Zen to be a lovesick old bachelor. So Dell had no fault to find with her. She and Zen could give away bicycles and auto-mobiles 'til doomsday and he would think that the last person in the world to object would be the person who was getting both as gifts. As far as he was concerned, he couldn't understand why I would rather go without a bicycle than have him make a fool of himself delivering it.

We were back at the leg-switching afternoon again. Then, he thought I'd endure something I didn't like to save him from being thought cruel. Now I was going to do the same thing again. Make such a fuss over his bicycle delivery that Miss Loomis would probably give it to him instead of me. Hadn't I thought of that?

Well, I had. And that would be fine with me.

Zen wanted me to look at the car. We had been talking about it for almost ten years. It was time for more than talk.

The car was down at Zen's garage, parked just outside his office like a vase of flowers. It was the best present he had ever given a woman. He didn't have enough money to give Love Lewis a gift that equaled his heart's love. Now with money and love in better balance, the woman seemed to doubt the validity of receiving such a gift.

He thought I was crazy. He knew all about the gift of a bicycle and Dell O'Dell's delivery of it.

"What's your objection?"

"After you and the Hup, Dell on the bike will look ridiculous."

"Does Dell think so?"

"No. He thinks he'll look good."

"He's a good rider. I've seen him."

"Not behind a Hup."

"I could destroy the Hup."

"You wouldn't!"

"No, I wouldn't. I've got too much sense for that. I was just making you a present. Not trying to outdo everything else on wheels in Valencia. Neither's Dell. Aunt Jetty, you disappoint me."

"Because I was trying to keep Dell from playing second fiddle?"

"Because you thought second fiddle mattered."

"Doesn't it?"

"Not unless you're running a race."

I could have said, "Well, aren't you?" But that was equal to asking him to declare himself. So I kept my mouth shut.

Zen declared himself, after a fashion, anyway.

"Let's take a ride," he said. "Hup now. Bike later. You can make up your mind which you like best."

"Uncle Zen, that's not the question. The question is, will you in a car make Dell on a bike look second-rate?"

"We know the answer to that. I will. Is that what this birthday is all about?"

I got in the car without another word. Zen didn't ask me which way I wanted to go. He headed toward the Santa Ana canyon. Since I'd said that water scared me, he'd take me where there was very little: the canyon with its little trickly river and Old Saddleback, a mountain, high and dry.

"At least you're not trying to mother me," said Zen. "Tell me what I should give you and what I shouldn't. At least you're not worried for fear I won't cut as good a figure as someone else. I appreciate that, Aunt Jetty."

Zen was being sarcastic and he knew I knew it. He was too concerned with the way I had acted to enjoy

167

demonstrating the car any longer. He pulled into a little driveway that led to the river, and turned off the engine.

"When going to school or looking after Neddie and Ramona gets too tiresome, the car will come in handy for a little escape like this," he said.

"And I better keep the key in my pocket or the person who escapes will be Neddie."

"Give him the bicycle. Now, let's forget cars, bicycles, and birthdays."

"We never used to talk of them."

Zen whipped those glasses he was never without from his pocket and put them once again on my nose.

"Who are you now?"

"Love Lewis."

"Who do you see?"

"Zenith McManus."

I couldn't say more. The specs on my nose, the lips on mine. The river with its quiet little summer whine. Behind the spectacles, my eyes were shut. Lips, without words, spoke to mine. And, wordless, mine replied.

That was my sixteenth birthday party. There beside the river with the car we had talked about for so many years.

18

Maybe I *was* acting like a mother to Dell. If so, I wasn't the mother Dell wanted.

He had already talked to Birdeen about being the delivery boy of a bicycle for Sarah Loomis. He wanted to know if Birdeen agreed with me. Would he look silly, pedaling in behind Zen in his fast flashy car?

Birdeen could have sent me out of the room while this conversation took place. Instead, she made me a part of it. It was easy to see why. She agreed with me.

"Dell," she said, "I can't exactly read Miss Loomis's mind. But maybe she thought that the sight of Zen in that flashy car making such a to-do out of presenting a teen-age niece with a birthday present needed to be compared with something more appropriate—teen-age boy on a bicycle?"

"You mean Uncle Zen is the silly one?" I asked, then added, "Maybe no one is silly."

"That's what I think," Dell said. "What's silly about giving the best you can afford as a present? I'd give Ginny a good bike if I had the money."

"Would you really, Dell? Not keep it for yourself?"

"No, and not have a public exhibition of how well I ride it, either."

"Like Uncle Zen? And the car?"

"Now, Ginerva," Mama said, "Dell isn't selling bicycles the way Zen is cars. There's nothing wrong with

Zen's killing two birds with one stone. Giving you a present and also letting people see what he's got for sale."

"The bicycle and me on it doesn't change any of that, does it, Mrs. Chalmers?"

"No," Birdeen answered reluctantly. "I guess it doesn't. No matter what Miss Loomis thinks. Thanks for coming over to talk to me about it, Dell. You deliver the bike. Ginerva will be glad to get it. Sarah will be glad to give it. And there's no reason why Zen should object to sharing a little of the limelight in the gift-giving business."

Birdeen started into the house. "There's cooking and cleaning has to be done, with or without birthdays. I need your help, Ginerva."

Dell got up to go just as Reno came in for dinner. What my father objected to wasn't Miss Loomis's bicycle. He didn't know anything about it. What he objected to was Zen and the Hup. In his opinion, Zen didn't make gifts to girls or women unless he expected a return of some kind.

I didn't know this about Zen. Of course, I did know that he was a ladies' man. I hadn't been a completely blind "little sweetheart" at four. And wearing the specs of Love Lewis at sixteen convinced me that nothing had changed except that the use of "little" in the sweetheart line was no longer appropriate.

Before Reno and Dell could get into any discussion of appropriate birthday gifts, I said good-bye to Dell and got my father into the dining room, where Ramona had set the table.

Reno said, "Ginerva, I hope you notice that while you were discussing how many birthday presents you should get, Ramona was busy helping."

Of course I noticed. We all did that. If one kid was in trouble, arguing with our parents or getting dressed-down for some wrongdoing, we—at least Neddie and I—put on a show of obedience and hard work. Ramona wasn't a show-off. She might have set the table just as fancy if there hadn't been any argument by big sister.

The combination—bicycle, Hupmobile, fancy table for the rancher, home from irrigating—set Reno's mind onto a subject he often thought about and talked about: that was the way times had changed since he was a boy.

"Here is Ginerva," he said, "in some kind of an argument about whether she should get both a bike and an auto. She should have lived forty years ago. When my father died, he didn't leave me even a penknife."

Birdeen came in then with the corn bread she had been baking.

"We know all about that missing penknife, Reno," she said. "Dinner's ready. Let's sit down now and return thanks."

Ramona was the thanks returner. She was sincere and she was short. Neddie counted while she prayed. When he got to fifty, he lifted his head and opened his eyes to show that, in his opinion, enough had been said.

Reno kept his head bowed for a long minute after Ramona had finished with the blessing. Still thinking, I believed, about the changed times: for him, no penknife; for me, more gifts than I knew what to do with.

After dinner, I cleared the table to make up for what I hadn't done before we ate. Reno stayed to talk to Birdeen.

"I've heard about Zen's gift of a car for Ginerva for so long I'm reconciled to that. But when did Sarah Loomis decide to get into the act? Why don't she ride the bike? Now, that would be a sight worth seeing."

"She probably don't ride it because she can't ride. Without risking an accident, anyway. She showed good sense getting Dell to do the riding," said Birdeen.

"Showed more than good sense, maybe."

"What do you mean, Reno?"

"Just an idea I had. It's too late now, but I'll be switched, Birdeen, if I understand how you ever said yes to Zen's Barnum and Bailey idea of driving his car in like a herd of trained elephants."

"He's been talking about it for ten years. I don't remember your ever objecting."

"I'm still not objecting. Just wondering about Loomis and the bicycle."

"You can stand two more days of wondering, I reckon."

"I reckon I can."

19

It wasn't the kind of birthday party I would have chosen, though except for the public presentation of bike and Hup, there was nothing unusual about it. Family and friends for a picnic supper. But after supper, the gifts, ending with Barnum Zen's and Bailey Dell's arrival with their trained steeds.

It was pretty show-off, no matter how you justified the Hup as a part of Zen's business, or the bike as an employer's appreciation of a faithful helper.

They, Zen and Dell, started down the lane that led to our house before the eating had finished. People stood in line with drumsticks in one hand and dill pickles in the other. This *was* half circus and half party.

Sarah Loomis headed for the front row, eager to see how her driver handled her gift.

Zen's outfit would have graced the Indianapolis Five Hundred. White pants, he must have gone clear to Los Angeles to buy. A blue coat with brass buttons that would have felt at home on a yacht. Nothing Dell could do on a bicycle could equal the figure Zen cut in the midst of his explosion of red and yellow.

People yelled as they started slowly down the lane. It might have been a horse race with the barriers just lifted.

Zen came at a moderate rate, necessitating Dell's dignified follow-up as a pedaler.

Dignified as long as it lasted. Dell started tailgating

very soon after he entered the lane. He had to. The Hup had slowed down and this, it seemed, in spite of the fiddling Zen was obviously doing with the throttle and choke.

The car evidently needed more than that. But this was no time to stop the car, lift the hood, and hunt breakdowns. The party guests forgot that they were at a party and thought they were at a race, a race in which the underdog was winning. They yelled encouragement to Dell.

Sarah Loomis, in the front row of onlookers at the lane, was about, it seemed, to rush out and give Dell an accelerating shove.

"Pass him, pass him," she yelled. "Show him what you can do. He's broken down. Go on around him."

Dell obviously had either to pass Zen or to get off his bike and push it at the snail's rate the Hup was making.

"Pass, pass," yelled Miss Loomis.

"Pass, pass," yelled the crowd.

Dell passed. Not like a strong kid on a new bicycle, but like a bullet hunting its victim.

When he reached the front lawn, he dismounted and waited for Zen.

It would be a long wait. Zen had stopped his ailing car and stood beside it like a mourner at the deathbed of a relation.

He was receiving all kinds of instructions, most of them sympathetic, from the onlookers.

"There's a lemon in every carload, Zen."

"Get a horse, Zen."

"Get a bike."

Sarah Loomis was speechless. She appeared flabbergasted. What had she expected? That Zen would lose his temper, shake his fist at Dell? Maybe accuse her of being responsible for his breakdown? Curse her?

If so, she was disappointed. As soon as the yelling and shouting of congratulations to the winner had died down, Zen mounted his car like a pulpit and shouted his own congratulations to Dell.

There wasn't an angry word in it. From anything Zen said, you would think he sold bikes, not Hups.

"There would be no automobiles today if there hadn't been bicycles first," he said. "And when you combine something as tested and proved as a bike with a rider as young and strong as Dell O'Dell, you have a winner. I congratulate my niece, who is receiving the bike as a gift from Miss Sarah Loomis. And I congratulate Miss Loomis, who anticipated the victory we have just witnessed."

When you're sixteen, at least when I was sixteen, a race between a bike and an auto doesn't seem a very satisfying way of celebrating your birthday. I suppose I understood that for most of the guests the party was over when the race was over.

The persons who were congratulated, as good-byes were said, were the drivers: Zen and Dell. Not me. Zen was congratulated, though he didn't win, for being such a gentleman. Dell, the winner, was appreciated for his determination and strong muscles.

When, at dusk, the last guest left, the family could say what it pleased to one another. Papa, usually the quiet one of the family, had a good deal to say.

"Birdeen," he said, "I hope you appreciated that

brother of yours today. I didn't know he had it in him."

"Had what in him?" Birdeen asked.

"The ability to face the kind of devilishness demonstrated by his girl friend, Sarah Loomis."

"I don't know what you're talking about, Reno."

"I don't think I need to explain that to you, Birdie. But after what somebody did to Zen's car, Sarah expected a real blowup from Zen. That's your brother's style, you know."

"Somebody did something? So that the car wouldn't run?"

"That's what they say down at the garage."

"Who would do such a thing?"

Birdeen wasn't capable of imagining such meanness, though it was easy for her to believe that her brother was capable of responding to such an act in the gentlemanly way he had. She always believed that Zen had a good side she alone saw, though only rarely.

Zen at once proved that his sister was right. He swept into the room, Sarah Loomis on his arm, and proudly announced his news.

"She had the nerve to do it. Boy! Am I proud of her!"

Boy! Was I ashamed of both of them. And still am. Miss Loomis was guilty of a criminal act; and Zen hadn't waited a minute to spread the news.

One thing I must say for Sarah Loomis. She understood Zen a lot better than his sister or his niece or his brother-in-law.

Reno probably thought Sarah Loomis was capable of the act she had, as a matter of fact, paid for. But he would never have admired it or praised it.

176

Zen admired it. He had had no idea that Sarah possessed enough grit for such an act. She wanted him to lose that race. She expected him to be a poor loser and, as such, to make a miserable spectacle of himself, cursing a poor kid; and demonstrating to the public the undependable merchandise he sold.

I had supposed that in the new car, Zen's gift to me, Zen and I would take a ride, a ride in which I would demonstrate my expertise as taught by him.

I couldn't do this in a car that wouldn't run. And Zen had other plans, anyway.

"Aunt Jetty," he said, "as soon as my car, I mean yours, is repaired, I want you to take me for a ride. Will you do that?"

All I could do was nod.

"Right now, Miss Loomis needs someone to drive her into town."

So that was the end of the ten-year plan for a car as soon as I learned how to drive. I almost suggested Zen pop Love Lewis's spectacles right smack on Sarah's nose. I wanted to say, "So Miss Loomis can see what Love saw." But that was too cruel. So I kept my tongue in my mouth and left the spectacles in his pocket. Zen and Miss Loomis drove off in her battered Maxwell without a word from the Chalmers tribe or Dell O'Dell. He, with the bicycle intended for me, felt like one of the family.

We hadn't said a word to Zen and Sarah and, for a long time, didn't speak to one another.

Then Reno said, "Dell, are you as good in an automobile as on a bike?"

"I never had any trouble with either," said Dell.

177

"You think you could manage my old Dodge?"

"If no one's tinkered with it."

"No one has. I can guarantee that. This party was supposed to end with Ginerva's ride in her new car. That's out of the question now. How about an old car with a new driver?"

"Me?" asked Dell.

"You," Reno said.

"Do you want to, Dell?" I asked.

"I want to," Dell said. "Let's go."

Birdeen said, "Reno, you're a genius."

She often forgot it, but that evening she hit the nail on the head. Reno was a genius. Dell was a darling, and I was a lucky birthday girl.

Neddie and Ramona thought so, too. They would never have dared volunteer to accompany Zen and me in the new Hup as passengers. They did more than volunteer with Dell O'Dell.

When Reno drove his Dodge to where we waited at the front of the house, Neddie and Ramona were already passengers, neat as peas in a pod in the back seat.

"Shall I unload them?" Reno asked Dell, who as driver would be responsible for them.

Dell looked at me. I was glad for their presence. They saved Dell and me from looking like a substitute for Zen and me. We were just family, out for an evening's jaunt in the family's old car.

"How about ice cream?" asked Dell.

Neddie, the eater, yelled, "Yes. I've got two bits."

The birthday party ended up at the Dairy Delight.

Vista
1921

Zen continued to have occasional breakdowns, but with better care, they lasted a shorter time. Sarah had moved in as his housekeeper. That's what she called herself. She was still postmistress. Mistress is what most people called her, ignoring the post office. President Harding wasn't a man who expected a post office to be run like a prayer meeting. Sarah and Mabel Osgood took the mail in and sent it out beyond anyone's complaining.

In the two years Sarah had been Zen's housekeeper, both had changed considerably—and for the better.

Zen, with Sarah's constancy in care and affection, seemed restored in body and spirit. Once again, he looked what he was: ten years Sarah's junior.

Though Sarah, by efforts of her own, had lopped years off that difference. The dumpy forty-six-year-old had become by the loss of about ten pounds an athletic thirty-five-year-old. The bicycle she had given me had become, little by little, hers. She could really ride it. She was no Dell O'Dell on a bike. But she didn't fall off or wobble.

She was never at ease when I was around. When I drove up in the Hup, which I kept shinier than the day I had received it, she usually, if at home, hopped on my ex-bike and pedaled off to the post office.

Zen reminded me not to consider her unsociable in doing so.

"You owe her a lot," Zen said.

"You, too," I said.

Zen laughed. "I admit it. You weren't cut out to be my housekeeper."

"Is that what you were thinking of when you called me your 'little sweetheart' and gave me an expensive car?"

"You know I wasn't."

"I didn't know it then."

"Sarah did."

"She's too smart for us. She knows something right now you don't know."

"Something you told her and didn't tell me? I'm hurt."

"No, no. Sarah knows that when I take the county teacher exam this summer and get my teaching credential, I'm going to marry Dell."

"Does Dell know it?"

I made such a jump at Zen, propped up with Enoch in his arms, that Enoch crossed the room in one long jump.

My intention had been to give Zen a good shake. "Of course Dell knows. Do you think I did the proposing?"

With Enoch out of the way and Zen's tanned face wrinkled somewhere between a smile and a laugh, a hug seemed more appropriate than a shake. I hugged him. And kissed him.

"You're kissing the bride," I said.

"I hope Dell doesn't mind."

"He thinks you're an old man."

"I thought so myself until Sarah came along. She thinks I'm a boy. You?"

What I thought of Zen was too complicated to put

into words. I didn't, of course, think Zen a boy—and never had. There had been times between the ages of four and eighteen when I dreamed of him as a husband. I doubt it was a dream Zen ever shared. "Little sweetheart" was as far as he went in that line.

I was able, as I snuggled into the curve vacated by Enoch, to understand more fully what Zen had said about the debt he owed Sarah.

Uncle and niece. Loving friends. Happy adventurers. But what I admired in the McManus line was all to be found in Birdeen. Mother and daughter, a relationship that was also filled with love and laughter and that wouldn't cause any eyebrows to be lifted.

Zen gave me a hug that Enoch resented. He landed with his twenty pounds in the inch of space between me and Zen. Zen rubbed him with his chin.

"Well, we've walked memory," I said. "Was it really like that? Is that the *was* that led to the *is*?"

"What do you think, Aunt Jetty?" Zen's tone still held the lightness of banter, but I sensed he was pointing me to something less than casual. "Suppose your traveling partner was Birdeen or Reno or Dell—would the view still seem the same?"

"Oh, Zen," I wanted to say, "how you wish your wayfaring companion could have been Love Lewis." What I did say was, "No. I suppose your partner makes the difference. Could even make the journey rough."

"Could do that. Better walk memory with someone who loves you, someone you love back."

"Do you remember telling me, a long time ago," I

asked Zen, "that Indiana town of Stony Lonesome was a place you wanted to avoid?"

"I called it a state. I've spent my life trying to avoid it. Sweethearts, wives, liquor, automobiles. I think I've finally made it. Lonesome no more. How could I be with Sarah, you, and Enoch? Where's my Stony Lonesome now?"

"Somewhere," I said, "but not here."